Jolted

Jolted

Newton Starker's Rules for Survival

Arthur Slade

 HarperTrophyCanada™
An imprint of HarperCollinsPublishersLtd

Jolted
© 2008 by Arthur Slade. All rights reserved.

Published by HarperTrophyCanada™,
an imprint of HarperCollins Publishers Ltd

HarperTrophyCanada™ is a trademark of HarperCollins Publishers.

First edition

HarperCollins books may be purchased for educational, business,
or sales promotional use through our Special Markets Department.

HarperCollins Publishers Ltd
2 Bloor Street East, 20th Floor
Toronto, Ontario, Canada
M4W 1A8

www.harpercollins.ca

Library and Archives Canada Cataloguing in Publication

Slade, Arthur G. (Arthur Gregory)
Jolted : Newton Starker's rules for survival / Arthur Slade. —1st ed.

ISBN: 978-0-00-639569-0

I. Title.

PS8587.L343J64 2008   JC813'.54   C2008-901847-8

WEB 9 8 7 6 5 4 3 2 1

Printed and bound in Canada.
Text design by Sharon Kish.
Illustrations on pages xi and 8 by Antonio Javier Caparo.

Jolted is printed on Ancient Forest Friendly paper,
made with 100% post-consumer waste.

For Mom and Dad,
who taught me not to play in a thunderstorm

Jolted

SURVIVAL THROUGH FIERCE INTELLIGENCE

Newton's Rules for Survival

1) Check the weather constantly.
2) Check the sky before exiting a building.
3) When thunder roars, run indoors.
4) Beware of cumulonimbus clouds.
5) Do not take a bath during a lightning storm.
6) Do not, under any circumstances, become angry. Count to ten. Breathe in. Breathe out.

Prologue:
The Reason Why He Always
Looked to the Heavens

Newton Starker knew he would most likely die from a lightning strike. The bolt would deliver three hundred kilovolts of electricity to the top of his skull, burning his scalp and popping thousands of brain cells like popcorn. Then it would arc along his nervous system, arteries, and veins, frying his heart and lungs. The lightning would leave deep burns at the exit points as it blew off his shoes and scraps of his clothing.

It would all happen in the blink of an eye. Zap! One fried fourteen-year-old, Newton, the last male heir of the Starker line.

Newton pressed his head back into his pillow and stared at the cracked paint on the dorm ceiling. His cot springs squeaked. Even here at the Jerry Potts Academy of Higher Learning and Survival, far from his home in Snohomish, Washington, he couldn't escape thinking about lightning. He would rather have been dreaming about girls or tasty new recipes, but his mind always reset to this: *A lightning bolt has my name on it.*

Lightning had blotted out nearly every member of the Starker family, including his grandfather, his Uncle Darwin, his mother. Sometimes it took more than one strike, but eventually they were smacked by a strong enough bolt.

Newton didn't believe the Starkers were cursed. No. Curses were illogical. He doubted it was a gene that attracted the lightning; the scientists at the University of Washington hadn't found a single suspect chromosome. It wasn't chance; it was statistically impossible for so many members of the same family to be hit by lightning. No one had any idea why it happened.

The only other Starker survivor was his Great-grandmother Enid, a woman who was as friendly as a pickled wolverine. He remembered each miserable visit his family had made to Great-grandmother. He'd rather have seen the dentist.

She was nothing like his mom. Delilah Starker had been warm and supportive and graceful. Newton swallowed the lump in his throat. It had been two years since the universe had dared to take her away.

I'm starting a new life, Mom. He sent this thought to the heavens. *Tomorrow it all begins. A school that will teach me how to survive. No one will laugh at a Starker again.*

He remembered the people who had teased him about his family's difficulties, people who had written blogs or newspaper articles or filled the airwaves with paranormal talk shows.

Pallbearers had carried his mother's coffin past a gaping crowd to the hearse. "Here comes the lightning!" someone had shouted. "Duck!" Remembering that, a giant worm of anger began to tie itself into knots in Newton's stomach.

He sat up in his cot, then stepped onto the hardwood floor. Wearing only his pyjamas and slippers, he sneaked down the back stairs of the junior boys' dorm, padded across the courtyard, and quietly opened the gate on the west wall of the Jerry Potts Academy. Being late August, a touch of the day's heat still hung in the air.

In moments he was standing on the flat prairie. The stars twinkled mischievously above him. He glared at the sky and raised his fist.

"Why? Why me? Why my family?" Then, with an emphatic finger poke, he growled, "I will win."

The hairs on the back of his neck began to rise. Were those cumulonimbus clouds skulking under the half moon? He thought he could just make out a telltale anvil shape blotting out the western sky, lumbering towards him.

"You don't scare me," he whispered, but he was trembling. *It's cold. That's why I'm shaking.*

A rumble in the distance. It had to be a train. Not thunder. Another low grumble made his heartbeat double. Then a flash.

He gave one last shake of his fist, bounded back to the dorm, took the stairs two at a time, and slid under the old army blankets on his cot. The rain began to fall, pelting at his window. He closed his eyes.

A full hour later he finally fell asleep.

Excerpt from *The Survival Handbook of the Jerry Potts Academy of Higher Learning and Survival*

Survival depends on your attitude. You must constantly be ready to stare down disaster. Exercise your body. Keep your mind fit. When that plane crashes, ship sinks, or train jumps its tracks, you will be the one to lead the other passengers to safety. Visualize success. Be prepared.

Always carry a sharp knife.

The Old, Odd School

The Jerry Potts Academy of Higher Learning and Survival sat like a fortress on the edge of Moose Jaw, Saskatchewan, Canada. The wolf's head crest howled eternally from the turret that rose above the iron gates. Through those gates, surrounded by a stone wall, was a stone church, a brick armoury, four brick classroom buildings, and three brick dorms. A brick belfry stood right behind the stone statue of Jerry Potts. The main office, in the centre of it all, was constructed of stone. The Academy exuded permanence and authority. Its Gaelic motto was "*Seasamh tro inntinn fraodh.*" Survival through fierce intelligence.

At 6:45 in the morning the belfry's bronze bell began to toll. Newton rubbed his eyes, crawled out of his cot, and splashed water on his face from the old metal sink in the corner of the room. The rusty taps seemed to be running water direct from the North Pole.

Newton's room was as plain as an army barracks, containing only a World War II–era cot, an ammunition box that served as a trunk, and a green aluminum closet. Pinned to the wall was a calendar of recipes, and a framed photo of Newton's dark-haired mother sat on the window ledge, her chalk-white skin glowing. Next to her photo was a framed drawing of a human hand, skin peeled back to reveal the tendons. It was his mother's work; she'd been a medical illustrator.

Get your thoughts together, Newton. This would be the first day of orientation, and he could barely figure out how to wear his uniform.

When Newton had arrived the night before, a ruddy-faced instructor, Mr. McBain, had checked off his name on a list, then tossed him a kilt and barked, "Welcome, laddie! You attach the right apron to the left buckle, the left apron to the waist and hip buckles, and the kilt comes to the centre of your knees, no farther. The sporran hangs three fingers below the waistcoat. If it's too low you'll get demerits. There's hose, flashes, and ghillie brogues. Wear them with pride, son. You get your *sgian dubh* tomorrow. Got that, laddie?"

Newton had understood only *welcome* and *laddie*. "Uh, yes, sir."

"Good. Now be off with you. Any fool can wear a kilt. I'm proof of that."

The Scottish uniform was the hallmark of the Jerry Potts Academy. Jerry Potts himself had been half Scottish. Kilts made it easier to wade through ponds or to swim, should a student have to dive fully clothed into a river to save a drowning companion or escape a herd of charging cattle. And the Academy got the kilts at a discount. Students could wear pants or regular clothes only during leisure time.

Newton held the red, green, and blue plaid kilt up in the light, trying to make sense of the belts and folds and pins. It was a Celtic jigsaw puzzle. As he tried to fasten it around his waist, several synapses sparked a memory.

A Shocking Array of Kilts

The memory that piped its way into his thoughts was of something that had occurred four years earlier. Newton, his mother, and his father had walked out of their geodesic dome home, climbed into their ancient Volvo station wagon, and driven from Snohomish, Washington, through the Rockies and the hills of Montana, to Moose Jaw, Saskatchewan. They had checked into the Temple Gardens Mineral Spa, then taken a deep collective familial breath and putted over to the Welakwa Home for the Elderly to visit Great-grandmother Enid Starker.

Within the first thirty seconds Enid had declared Newton "small enough that one static shock would obliterate him" and then referred to Newton's father, Geoffrey, as "the dome-headed wonderboy." His head was slightly bald.

"We're not wanted here," Geoffrey said to Delilah and Newton.

"You're not wanted anywhere," Enid cackled.

"Well, I didn't drive all this way to be insulted by an ungrateful prune."

"Ouch!" Enid crinkled her face. "At least this prune has personality."

"Time out!" Delilah shouted. She grabbed her husband and son and dragged them to the lobby. "We're going for a drive to cool off."

After checking the sky to be sure the weather hadn't changed, they piled into the car and drove aimlessly around Moose Jaw.

"Let's go home," Geoffrey hissed.

"Dad's right," Newton said from the back seat.

"No!" Delilah said. "Both of you, be patient. Enid's mean and angry but apart from Newton she's the only blood relative I've got."

Geoffrey was silent. The spot on the top of his head that turned crimson when he was perturbed gradually cooled to pink. "I'm not dome-headed, am I?"

"Not even in the slightest." Delilah rubbed his shoulder.

That's when they spotted the Jerry Potts Academy of Higher Learning and Survival.

Geoffrey cranked the wheel, shot up the driveway, slammed on the brakes, and leaped out of the car. "Gothic Revival. That's got to be Tyndall stone. Tyndall stone!" he shouted, pointing at the main building. "The cream-coloured mottling is evidence of prehistoric burrowing marine creatures. If we got up close we'd see fossils trapped in the limestone. But that's not all, look at the tracery!" Geoffrey was a structural engineer and tended to get excited about such things.

Delilah spun in her seat and clutched Newton's shoulder. "Not safe," she whispered. Her eyes (one blue, one grey) narrowed. "The sky is never, ever safe. There's a cloud out there.

I see it hiding just beyond the school walls. If there's lightning the car will protect us. Lightning will travel down the sides and into the earth. Just don't touch the door handles."

"I know, Mom," Newton said sniffily. "It's rule number seven: *The interior of the car is safe, but don't touch any metal parts.*"

She squeezed his shoulder gently. "Good boy."

Newton was impressed by the sense of permanence that the Jerry Potts Academy projected. This compound could stand up to a severe thunderstorm. Even a cyclone. On the steeply pitched roof of the central building several sword-shaped lightning rods stuck up into the sky like points on a crown.

Then, as though they'd been waiting for the Starker family's arrival, the front gates opened and out marched a regiment of senior students in kilts, their sporrans and clan pins bright in the sun. Bagpipes were squealing. It was such a shocking array of kilts that Newton gaped.

"Ah, bagpipes!" his mother said. "Good for what ails the MacStarker heart. A shame we dropped the 'Mac' from our name."

To which Newton responded in a barely audible whisper, "One day, this will be my school."

Meanwhile, Back at the Kilt Buckle

It took a few attempts to fasten them. Newton consulted his student manual and adjusted his sporran—the brass-plated pouch with a broom of horsehair—so that it hung over his belly button. He pulled his hose up to his knees and slipped his feet into the ghillie brogues, high-laced brown shoes with extra-grip soles for climbing. He smoothed out the wrinkles in his white dress shirt and added a waistcoat, a black argyle jacket, and a bow tie. The bow tie was impossible to knot neatly. Neckties had been banned by the Academy because they interfered with outdoor activities. A few students had been using them to snare ground squirrels.

The kilt seemed secure. Newton gazed into the speckled mirror on his door. It looked as though a blind clown had dressed him. His mother had always said he was handsome "in an Edgar-Allan-Poe kind of way." That meant he was pale and his hair was dark, like hers.

One eye was sky blue, the other a cloudy grey. Mismatched eyes was a Starker family trait. He liked to think his eyes made him look older than fourteen and, maybe, a little spooky.

Thinking of the Starker rules, he flipped open his laptop and went to the weather page. Sun and clear skies and no chance of rain or thundershowers. He was safe. And he was late! He scooted down the stairs and outside, all the while feeling the cool on his bare legs. He joined the orientation class.

"Ach, good of you to finally show up, laddie," Mr. McBain shouted. He was short, built like a bulldog, and had bristly grey hair. He had shouted his way through private school in Buckie, Banffshire, Scotland, then shouted himself up to the rank of sergeant in the British Army, then shouted out a position in the Special Air Service. He'd shouted his way across every continent, through several death-defying missions, then shouted, "Ach! I'm retiring!" Finally he'd shouted himself into a position as an instructor at the Jerry Potts Academy.

All fifty-two grade nine students were clad in their kilts. Some had fastened them expertly; others kept their hands on their belts, expecting gravity to play a prank. They all turned as one to stare at Newton. The faces were male, female, black, white, Asian—a mix of intelligent and sleepy. Newton was relieved when they turned their attention back to Mr. McBain.

"We shall visit the mess, where there's haggis for breakfast," Mr. McBain announced. Several students groaned. "What? Groaning! There's nothing better than heart and liver minced with onion and boiled in the stomach of a sheep. It has a delectable nutty flavour! And it'll put hair on your chest. Except you gals; it'll make you taller. Anyway, I jest—haggis is for dinnertime. After your morning gruel we shall conduct a tour of the library, the stables, and your classrooms." He paused. "But first, the annual McBain Poetry Spout-Off!"

Students exchanged curious glances and murmurs. Mr. McBain led them to the Highland Courtyard. They followed like a tartan amoeba. Newton worked his way to the front of the pack.

Mr. McBain stopped before the Orator's Perch, a large, bench-like stone that a farmer had found sixty years before. "Now! It's poetry time. Since we appreciate the arts so much here at Jerry Potts, one of you lads or lassies will do the honour of reciting my favourite Scots poet, Robbie Burns. And no 'Auld Lang Syne'—that makes my eyes all watery. Whoever is brave enough to stand up here will receive extra marks in my culinary class."

Here's my chance! Newton searched the sky for cumulonimbus clouds, then jumped up to the flat part of the stone, his hand holding his kilt. In eighth grade he had memorized "A Red Red Rose."

"O my Luve's like a red, red rose, That's newly sprung in June," he began. Everyone was staring at him, some bored, others, he assumed, with envy. Maybe he would impress the girls. He put his heart and his lungs into the recitation, bringing it to a dazzling conclusion by lifting both his hands and practically shouting, "And I will come again, my Luve, Tho' 'twere ten thousand mile!"

A hard object struck his left kilt buckle. He turned to see who had thrown it and briefly locked eyes with a tall Asian girl. She was giggling and pointing, standing right next to Mr. McBain, who looked grim. It was obvious to Newton that the girl had been the catapult. He opened his mouth to point out that she was being rude just as his left buckle unsnapped and his kilt dropped.

Newton was wearing bright-green undershorts. The students' laughter roared like a thundercloud.

"'at's why we tighten our buckles!" Mr. McBain shouted. "You canna meet the Queen with a kilt obscene! Leave the lad to fix it. On to the mess, you ugly mob."

Newton pulled up his kilt and tried to reattach the buckles while everyone else followed Mr. McBain to the old armoury.

"Do you want advice?"

Newton, startled, turned to see a brown-skinned, blue-eyed boy smiling up at him. His eyes swam behind thick spectacles.

"Advice? This kilt is broken."

"Oh, they're all rather tricky. You've got to fasten the right apron to the left buckle." He pretended to do up his own kilt. Newton followed his lead. "That's it," the boy said. "The left apron attaches to your waist and hip buckles. You're stylin' now!"

Newton was surprised at how tight and sturdy the kilt felt. "How do you know how to do this?"

"I'm Scottish."

"Huh?"

The boy laughed. "Part Scottish. And part Mi'kmaq, and African-American, too, but it's a long story." He reached out his hand. "My name's Jacob."

15

Jacob's Story in a Nutshell

Jacob Edward Clarke was fourteen and from Halifax, Nova Scotia. His mother was from the Mi'kmaq First Nations tribe, his father was black. In 1857, his father's ancestors had escaped to Canada on the Underground Railroad for slaves. His grandmother had been Scottish. He wasn't certain with which bloodline he should identify, so he chose to honour all of them.

The Hall of Heroes

The moment Jacob and Newton began to shake hands, Jacob got a shock.

"Ouch!"

"Oh, sorry," Newton said. Jacob looked at his hand as though he expected a few fingers to be blown off. "I store a lot of static electricity. It's part of my condition."

Jacob stuck his hand out again, this time to help Newton down from the Orator's Perch. There was no shock. Newton jumped.

"Condition?" Jacob asked.

"It's a long story. I'm Newton Starker." He paused, waiting for Jacob to recognize his name. He assumed everyone was familiar with his electrical history, but Jacob didn't react. Maybe they didn't get the news up here in Canada.

"How about we have some breakfast?" Jacob said.

They walked towards the hulking armoury, where the doors were gulping up the last of the ninth-grade crowd.

"So what brings you here?" Newton asked.

"My father wants me to toughen up." Jacob pushed his glasses back up his nose. "And I need to work on my writing. The Academy has a great arts program."

"Oh, you write?" *Maybe he'll want to write my life story.* "What kind of writing?"

"Fantasy." Jacob reached into his backpack and pulled out a book. He pressed it into Newton's hand. "Here, read my latest. It's called *The Brilliad*. I published it myself."

The book was heavy as a brick, leather-bound, and on its cover was a square maze.

"Wow." Newton flicked it open. "Yeesh, that's tiny print."

"To keep printing costs down, I had to use a smaller font. The ideas were just bursting out of my head. And I'm almost finished my next one."

"That's great!" *He must be a genius.* Newton hoped Jacob would ask why he'd come to the Academy. When he didn't, Newton volunteered, "I came because I'm very much into surviving, but I'm also a chef. Or, at least that's what I'd like to become."

"A chef? Cool. I like eating."

They walked into the armoury, passing through a long hall with glass cases on either side. A group of kilted seniors marched by looking like Celtic deities, their cheeks rosy. The guys laughed with deep voices; the girls' laughter was light and tantalizing. *Soon, I'll be as confident as them.*

"This is the Hall of Heroes," Jacob said. "That's what I read in the pamphlet, anyway."

They stopped at a display case featuring photographs of those who had graduated and had gone on to worldwide acclaim, including scientists, actors, generals, and explorers. The largest photo was of Wilhelm Duggs, the lion-tamer.

Next to the pictures hung a shield-shaped bronze plaque listing the students in each grade who'd had the highest year-end marks, going back eighty years.

"That's where I want *my* name to be," Newton whispered. He stared at the plaque as if trying to etch his name with laser vision.

"Ah, the mighty always aim high," Jacob replied.

Was Jacob making fun of him? Or maybe he just talked like that because he was a writer. *He thinks I'm mighty.*

Next to the plaque was a long corkboard with several notices pinned to it about basketball, boxing, and extracurricular community activities. A list of students' marks from the previous year was tacked up, right in the middle.

They turned left into the mess and lined up for their "slop." The cook had a glass eye and her hands were yellowed with nicotine stains. She muttered and grumbled. Newton decided he'd never discuss recipes with her.

He sat at one of the many folding tables. The porridge tasted like five-week-old haggis cooked in a bagpipe. Clearly the Academy's cook had failed to call upon her inner chef. Even a few raisins would have piqued Newton's gastronomical interest. *They would have been a* raisin d'etre. He chuckled to himself. *If only the world could see inside my brilliant brain.*

Jacob slid into the chair across from him, an orange, a muffin, and a cup of tea on his tray.

Newton experienced a sudden and, for him, mostly unfamiliar feeling: he was sure he and Jacob were going to become friends.

The *Starkers' Friend Policy*

Newton wasn't good at making friends. For one thing, he was rather quiet. For another, people could sense his inner oddness a light-year away. It wasn't hard to follow this new policy because he didn't have any friends. That was thanks, in part, to his mother. Delilah had constructed a special lightning-deflecting tinfoil hat and made him wear it through all the junior grades (he'd left it at home this time because he knew how important first impressions would be at a new school).

Many of the girls at his former middle school thought he was "the quiet cutie who was most likely to turn into an axe-murderer." Why else would his eyes be two different colours?

The guys just found him weird.

Newton had been taught that it was his social responsibility to not make friends. It was dangerous for others to get too close to a Starker; sometimes lightning struck those nearby. His mother was proof of that.

Seven years ago, Delilah had officially instituted the *Starkers' Friend Policy*. She had been with her best friend, Margaret. They had taken about three steps outside one of the antique shops in Snohomish when Delilah looked up to see clouds unspooling in the sky. A bolt struck her and she spent a week unconscious in Seattle's Northwest Hospital.

Margaret was killed. Not by the lightning; it just knocked her out. But when she fell, she struck her head on the post of a faux-antique street lamp and died instantly.

Newton's mother had always been bubbly and eager to laugh, but after Margaret died, Delilah would slip into long periods of grumpiness and glare out her home-office window. "It should have been me," she would whisper, over and over. She drew fewer and fewer medical illustrations and eventually stopped taking assignments altogether. Even some of the delectable dishes Newton made didn't seem to cheer her up. They had always cooked together. And the Starkers did have especially sensitive tastebuds.

After Margaret's death, Delilah had decided it wasn't safe for Starkers to have friends. They could die. And besides, friends were a lot of work. Friends expected you to leave your dome and shop for antiques. Or attend their parties.

"It'll be better for you, Newton, if you don't make friends," his mother had said. "You'll always, always have me. I promise."

Ad Nauseam

Newton left his porridge uneaten. Whatever the rest of orientation morning dealt him, he'd have to face it on an empty stomach. "This is nauseatingly bad porridge."

"Right. Good word, too," Jacob said.

Across the room the Asian girl stood up, apparently having finished her breakfast. "Who's that really tall girl?" Newton asked, pointing discreetly.

"Violet Quon. Miranda, the girl with the pink hair, knows her from summer camp. She said she's a cannibal."

"What?"

"I assume she was joking. I think she meant she's a carnivore. Miranda's a vegan."

Newton shot an angry glance at Violet. "She's the one who made my kilt fall. She threw something at me."

Jacob scratched his temple. "Really? I didn't see that. But if you'd like my advice, it's best to rewrite these experiences in your mind. I re-imagine them turning out well. You should just visualize that kilt staying up."

"You're right. Visualization! I'm visualizing my revenge right now."

"That's not exactly what I meant."

Without another word Newton picked up his tray and carried it towards the collection cart, crossing Violet's path. At exactly the right moment he flipped his tray and his porridge landed on her kilt, sticking like glue.

"Nice move, clumsy," she said, wiping the crud from her kilt. She was exceedingly tall; a good six inches taller than Newton.

"Ha!" He laughed. "It's payback."

"For what?" She squeezed a handful of porridge and Newton prepared to duck.

"Don't play innocent," he said. "I'm not to be messed with."

"You're confused. Maybe your green undershorts are too tight."

"Shut up about my shorts!" This he said a little too loudly. Chuckles rang in his ears.

Violet stepped closer and looked down her nose at him. "I don't know what game you're playing, but I know who you are, Newton Starker. I read up on all my classmates. You've flipped porridge on the wrong Quon."

"Hmmmph." *What a lousy comeback.* "Yeah, right."

She gave him a withering glare, then stalked off to the washrooms.

He put his tray away, trying to act calm, in case other students were still watching. He breathed through clenched teeth. *I should have counted to ten!* His hands balled up into fists.

"Don't let the Starker anger get the best of you." His mother had said it a million times. "Count to ten. Wait. Master it."

He let out his breath. It was okay. This little incident was nothing.

Sheep's Pluck and
His Very Own *Sgian Dubh*

That evening there was a short ceremony after dinner, which was, as promised, haggis. Newton swallowed several small bites. Mr. Dumont, the headmaster, stood on a platform at the far end of the mess hall. He wore a lumberjack shirt, his chest big as a whisky barrel. Several lash-like scars lined his bearded face.

"Welcome to the Jerry Potts Academy of Higher Learning and Survival." His voice was so deep and strong it could have split atoms. "Tonight we especially welcome our newest batch of survivors into grade nine. I'd like to call them up to the platform."

"What's this about?" Newton whispered to the boy next to him.

"We're getting our *sgian dubhs*."

When Newton gave him a blank look the boy said, "Knives. Traditional Scottish knives. Your parents must have signed the consent form."

"I guess so," Newton replied.

Three senior pipers—one girl with bright-red hair and two tall boys—piped the ninth grade to the stage. Each student was called up to receive the *sgian dubh*. Newton took his carefully and pulled the dark blade an inch from its sheath. It was serrated on one side. He couldn't imagine any school in the United States that would actually arm its students. Jerry Potts Academy was cool!

Mr. Dumont looked down on them all. "This *sgian dubh* is entrusted to you to be worn upon your person at all times. If any of you misuse it, especially in a threatening manner, you will immediately be expelled. You are now officially members of the Jerry Potts Academy. Sleep well. Tomorrow you will learn how to use the *sgian dubh*. Until then, it remains sheathed. And remember—always keep your knives sharp."

From: headmasterdumont@jerrypottsacademy.com

Date: Thursday, August 29

Subject: Start of First Quarter

To: allgradesaddresses

Dear Students,

Welcome. Tomorrow, classes begin. You are expected to arrive on time and to be properly dressed in your school uniform. Anyone who does not meet the standards will receive demerit points. Be prepared to learn. This is an intense educational experience. Each quarter is only ten weeks long.

The following are messages of importance:

1) Mr. McBain reminds the grade nine students that next Tuesday, in Fine Culinary Arts class, you will create a main dish from a surprise meat that he will provide. You are responsible for an original recipe, seasonings, and any other items needed. It will be worth 15% of your culinary mark. Purchase your own materials in town (preferably at the Co-op) or ask for them from Mess Cook Norquay.

2) Grade ten students are entailed with stable duty this quarter. The manure truck arrives on Saturday at 10:00 a.m. Bring your rubber boots. There will be plenty of pitchforks and shovels available.

3) Books borrowed from the library must be returned on the due date. If you are late you will be assigned stable duty.

4) The first-quarter Outdoor Expedition will begin on September 18. It will be an arduous forty-hour survival challenge that will test all that you've learned in your first weeks. Not every student has been able to complete the Expedition. Those who fail are sent home. It counts for 25 percent of your total mark. Begin visualizing success now.

I am pleased to have so many returning students as well as new faces. Remember, we are a community. Work together, learn together, survive together.

Sincerely,
Mr. Dumont, Headmaster

P.S. Our bell-ringer this week will be grade eleven student Arden Henry. Arden decided the dress code didn't apply to him during our dinner meal. Learn from Mr. Henry's mistake. The staff at Jerry Potts Academy are extremely observant. We see everything.

Newton's First-Quarter Classes

Mercantile Fitness and Survival 9
Six weeks of intensive study of financial matters, including operating a small business, combined with outdoor survival training concentrating on observation of habitat and building survival shelters. The survival training will mould you into an enterprising CEO or entrepreneur.

Biology and Survival of the Fittest 9
In this course, you will study biology that is relevant to your life. Curriculum will follow The Nature of Life, Ecology, Cells, Evolution, Micro-organisms and Fungi, Plants, Invertebrates, Chordates, and The Human Body. The survival aspect will include a study of how to avoid predators and how to become a predator.

Literature and Communication 9
This intensive study of communication will include analyzing propaganda, understanding advertising, learning the structure of the novel (including in-depth reading of *To Kill a Mockingbird* and *Lord of the Flies*), composition, public speaking, and debating. You will be taught hand signals, Morse code, and smoke signals to be used in a survival situation.

Culinary Arts and Survival 9

This class is designed to debunk the taboos regarding food that civilization has instilled in you. In a survival situation your only goal is to consume the number of calories needed to maintain life. This class will teach you which animals and animal parts are edible, and which insects and plants should be consumed and which are poisonous. Outdoor activities will include techniques for trapping, gathering, and cooking. No matter what materials are used, you are expected to approach cooking with artistry and imagination.

Ethics of Survival 9

This half-credit course, mandatory for all students, is about the taboos and misconceptions that surround survival. Is survival for the "fittest"? Is it "every woman for herself"? If one mountain climber has slipped and is pulling down several other climbers, do you cut the rope? Here we will ask the hard questions and answer them.

Boxers or Briefs?

The following morning, the bell in the belfry tower bonged at 6:45 a.m. Newton shot out of his cot and splashed water on his face.

He carefully fastened the right apron of his kilt to the left buckle, then attached the left apron to his waist and hip buckles. He'd practised before going to bed. His stomach was fluttering. *I'm nervous,* he thought. *I, Newton Starker, am nervous.*

It was August 30, the first day of classes, and from this moment forward he wanted to perform perfectly. He'd gotten off to a bad start on orientation day, but he could turn the *Good Ship Starker* around. He had graduated from Montessori with distinction and had repeated this feat at Centennial Middle School. But here at Jerry Potts, with students from across the world, he was among the best of the best.

Ya canna meet the Queen with a kilt obscene! Mr. McBain had shouted at him. It was now Newton's mantra. *I can't have another kilt drop.*

Today, Newton wore silk boxers, just in case. Boxers, at least, were cool. And they were monogrammed with *NGS:* Newton Goddard Starker.

He adjusted his sporran so that it hung the regulation three fingers below his waistcoat.

The last item he attached to his person was his *sgian dubh*. He slid it into the sheath belted around his right sock.

A buzzing echoed in Newton's ears, like a thousand mosquitoes hovering a few microns away. *Oh, it's gonna be one of those days*, he thought. Sometimes he could actually hear the electricity zapping its way through the wires in the walls. The University of Washington scientists had told him it was his imagination, but Newton knew better. It was a Starker thing.

"We're plugged into the universe," his mother used to say. "Whether we like it or not."

At least it was a low hum. Newton knew it didn't necessarily mean anything bad was on the way, but he glanced outside anyway. The arrow-slit window revealed the sun rising into an innocent blue sky. No lightning today. Not trusting his eyes completely he flipped open his MacBook, surfed to the weather page. Sunny. Safe! He could dare the outdoors.

A flashing icon appeared on his iChat. He clicked it and his father's face filled the screen. Geoffrey Slights smiled.

"Newton. I was hoping I'd catch you. Just want to wish you luck on your first day of school."

"Thanks, Dad. But I don't need luck—I need good grades."

Newton could tell that his father was at the Millennium Domes office because he was sitting in front of the massive poster of a monolithic dome he'd designed and built.

"Hey, don't forget to have fun, too!" His father's cellphone chirruped in the background. "I've got to go. We're putting up another dome in Marysville. It's going to be a school."

"Congrats! Oh, and thanks for the pep talk, Dad."

"No prob, homeboy." It always irked Newton when his father tried to sound cool. "Oh, and don't forget to visit your great-grandmother. Your mother would've wanted you to."

Newton rolled his eyes. "I will. I will."

Out of habit, he checked the weather again. Still safe. He resisted the urge to check it a third time. He thought of his father, sitting in his office, not one bit worried about the weather. *Would my life have been different if I'd been given his last name?*

Why Newton's Dad's Last Name Was Slights

It was his family name.

His father didn't pass his last name on to Newton because when he married Newton's mother he agreed to respect the Starker tradition requiring anyone with Starker genes to keep the surname. Some had changed it, hoping to avoid being struck. They'd died by lightning anyway.

The Starkers were stubborn. They were proud. Let the universe try and wipe them all out. It couldn't obliterate the Starker name.

Newton's dad was allowed to choose Newton's given names: Newton, in honour of Sir Isaac Newton, and Goddard, in honour of Robert Goddard, the father of rocketry.

One final point about Geoffrey Slights: he loved eggs Benedict. And the best version he'd ever had was made by his son.

Newton Goddard Starker's Amazing Eggs Benedict Recipe

Eggs Benedict (or eggs Benny) is the only civilized breakfast/brunch for a Sunday morning.

First separate two eggs. Break the yolks and add a cup of milk, a half teaspoon of salt (be precise!), and 1½ cups of flour. Add a tablespoon of melted butter (real butter! I mean it! You'll be disappointed otherwise). Beat it like crazy. Then add two tablespoons of baking powder (not baking soda!) and fold into the well-beaten whites. Bake on a griddle in large muffin rings.

Broil some good ham. Make a hollandaise sauce (I use tarragon vinegar, that's the old way) and cut up a truffle (preferably plucked from the fertile ground of France), and poach the required number of eggs.

Pop the muffins from their rings. Place a square of ham on each, then a poached egg, and cover with hollandaise sauce (be generous). Dust with truffle and serve immediately.

This dish cannot sit around.

There is no better egg recipe.

Proof that Two Objects Cannot Occupy the Same Space at the Same Time

Newton smiled. His hair was particularly staticky today and it took a goopy load of gel to keep it down, but that aggravation didn't affect his mood. He was going to get a perfect mark in his *Culinary Arts and Survival 9* class on mystery-meat day.

He'd gone through his massive list of recipes and a truffle quiche had leaped out at him. Of course, it required real truffles. Only Newton would be able to pull it off. Others would try Szechuan something-or-other or lasagna. *Ha. How unimaginative! I'll put the* scrump *in* scrumptious.

Newton imagined his classmates' awe when he pulled the dish from the oven. Afterwards they wouldn't point and say, "Isn't that the kid whose family gets hit by lightning?" Instead they'd say, "There's that guy who made the best dish I ever tasted. The world owes him."

Once Mr. McBain had tried Newton's quiche, he'd never eat haggis again.

Newton slung his backpack over his shoulder, ran down the dorm steps, opened the door into the Great Hall of Chief Piapot, and took a step, all the while dreaming of his brilliant recipe.

A dark shadow flitted across his peripheral vision, but before he could react he felt a sharp blow to his side and he was knocked, sprawling, to the floor, with his papers fluttering around like giant moths.

A girl was folded up like human origami beside him. She unfolded, spider-like, and pushed herself to a sitting position. The moment she saw it was Newton, her eyes narrowed.

"Nice hip check, Rod," Violet growled, her small teeth sparkling between thin lips. Her long, dark hair was in a tight, stiff braid, her dress shirt was crisp, and her kilt fit perfectly. She stood up, holding one of Newton's papers, then dropped it as though it carried the plague. "When you grow up you could become a speed bump, Rod."

"Why are you calling me Rod?" Newton demanded. "I'm Newton."

"You'll figure it out some day, Rod."

Newton gathered his papers, crushed them to his chest, and launched himself to his feet. He was six inches shorter than Violet, but he stood on his tiptoes, shot her his most virulent look, and spat out, "Your bow tie is crooked."

"Your eyes are crooked." Violet grinned, spun on her heel, and strode across the Great Hall.

Newton *was* slightly cross-eyed. He glared, wishing a piano would fall out of the sky and crush her into *sauce de Violet*.

A Few Unimportant Facts About Violet

1. She was a third-generation Chinese-Canadian. Her great-grandfather was a semi-famous photographer who took pictures of prospectors and saloon girls in the Yukon during the gold rush.
2. She brushed her teeth after every meal and before bed. She carried the toothbrush in the pouch of her sporran.
3. She played the oboe.
4. Her father was a Mountie stationed in Nanaimo, British Columbia.
5. Her twin brother, Vernon, who went to school at Nanaimo Central High School, was spoiled. In her opinion. He always got higher marks. Always got the better slice of steak. Always got on her nerves. That's why she asked to come to the Jerry Potts Academy. And because she wanted to be a Mountie, just like her father.
6. Her father graduated from Jerry Potts. His name was listed in the Hall of Heroes.
7. Violet intended to see her name on the same plaque.

The Odyssey Across the Square

Newton pushed open the doors to the Highland Courtyard and looked up. Three clouds hovered above him, white and wispy cartoon characters with a shade of darkness on their lower edges. *Death is waiting in our bowels*, they whispered. By their shape he knew they weren't even rain- or lightning-bearing, but he still hated them. It was something in the way they just floated there, taunting him. He sucked in a noseful of air. Not enough moisture or crackling in his ears to worry. He was safe.

He strolled along the sidewalk next to the junior girls' dorm, his kilt fluttering in the breeze. The building was yet another brick, three-storey fortress, with arrow-slit windows that looked over the prairies on one side and, in the opposite direction, Moose Jaw. Gargoyles along the roof gazed out at the horizon, waiting for winter.

Newton examined the lightning rods on top of the building. Headmaster Dumont had told Newton's father that the Academy had invested in several new ones after accepting Newton as a student. He turned back to look at the massive boys' dorm, where the rods stuck out of the heads of two wolf statues. They had already been blackened by lightning that had tried to get in while he'd been sleeping. The rods were connected to a cable that carried the lightning away from the building and down into the ground.

Newton carried on past the stone statue of Jerry Potts. He admired the man for surviving on the harsh prairie wearing buffalo skins and a derby hat. If that didn't deserve respect, then nothing did.

The Amazing Life Story of Jerry Potts

Jerry was a Wild Canadian West character.

In the 1830s, his Scottish father, Andrew Potts, worked for the American Fur company at Fort Mackenzie on the Upper Missouri. He married Crooked Back, a Blackfoot woman, and Jerry the Métis was born. Sadly, Andrew was shot by a Piegan Indian who'd thought he was shooting a different white man (white men do tend to look the same). Jerry was only two years old at the time, so after a couple of stepfathers came and went, he was raised by the manager of the fort. He became a crack shot, picked up several Indian languages, and returned to his Blackfoot tribe to learn to track and hunt. He was given the name Kyi-yo-Kosi (Bear Child). He proceeded to avenge his father's death and his mother's death and his stepbrother's death. This is what historians refer to as his Revenge Period.

Later in life he guided the North West Mounted Police across the prairies and scouted for the Canadian army during the 1885 Riel Rebellion. His tracking abilities became legendary. He could adapt to any situation and nothing could kill him. Well, almost nothing. Throat cancer got him in 1896. Apparently, smoking was bad for you in the old days, too.

Leaving aside his tobacco habit and his love of whisky, he was the perfect person after whom to name a Canadian private school. He'd survived by virtue of his fierce intelligence.

Potts had never worn a kilt, but that didn't prevent the masters of the school from insisting that every student wear one. He had been half Scottish, after all. And there was nothing tougher than a Scot in a kilt.

Meanwhile, Newton Had Moved On to the Breakfast Table

"Struggling through your morning brekkie, I see," Jacob said as he sat down with a bowl of steaming goo on his tray. "Cogitated any brilliant thoughts lately?"

Newton ran this question around in his brain a couple of times and considered the possibility that Jacob might be mocking him. One look at Jacob's friendly face laid that worry to rest.

"Yes!" Newton said, so loudly that Jacob jumped. Newton bit his lip, deciding it might be wiser to keep his recipe a secret.

"Yes, what? You sound excited!"

"I am!" In fact, exuberance fairly fizzed up inside him like a bottle of well-shaken pop. "I came up with something completely and utterly original."

"A vision from beyond, the great gleam," Jacob said, as though quoting poetry. "What was it?"

"Okay, okay, I'll tell you." Newton leaned forward and spoke in a hushed tone. "I'm going to make a truffle dish for Culinary Arts class. Truffles!" He waited for Jacob's jaw to drop in awe. "Isn't that an amazing idea?"

"Truffles? Chocolates and mystery meat?"

"No! No! The fungus! France's greatest export. Black truffles! They sell for hundreds of dollars an ounce."

Jacob raised his hands. "Hold your horses, Newton. I know what they are. They use pigs to find them, right? It sounds like a good idea."

"Good? Truffles are brilliant! I tell you, this could be one of those really pivotal moments in my history."

"You sound like Caesar. *I came. I saw. I truffled.*"

"Exactly!" Newton beamed. "Though I do tend to model myself more after Napoleon, sans Waterloo. Caesar bloomed kind of late. Anyway, all I have to do is order the truffles."

"Go for it!" Jacob reached across and gave Newton a celebratory slap on his shoulder.

Newton found himself suddenly teary. No one, other than his parents and a fencing coach at Centennial School, had ever given him a sincere pat on the back. Everyone else was too worried about getting a shock.

"I—I can't wait," Newton said. "As a writer, you may want to document this early part of my career. I was born to be a chef."

"Uh . . ." Jacob rubbed his jaw as though searching for stubble. "Your life story does have a certain appeal, but I'm a little busy. I've got to get my second fantasy novel out to the publishers. I've entitled it *Phantasmic Armies.*"

"Wow," Newton said. The previous night, he'd read part of Jacob's first novel, *The Brilliad.* The whole book was one sentence that lasted a thousand pages. It had hurt Newton's brain. *Say something positive about his writing,* Newton told himself, but nothing came to mind.

Luckily, at that moment, a low, ominous *bong* filled the room and Newton exclaimed, "Better get moving. Time for class."

How Newton First Discovered Truffles

When Newton was eleven, his family was invited to Michael Skrypuch's brand-new house. Newton's father had designed and built the home, which was composed of four interlocked domes and a dome garage. It looked like a moonbase.

An elderly butler lowered a plate of hors d'oeuvres before Newton. There were seven star-shaped crackers on the plate, each spread with a film of truffle butter. When he placed one in his mouth, Newton's tastebuds exploded with joy.

"What. Is. This?" he asked.

The butler smiled and whispered, *"Monsieur, c'est* heaven."

Later that evening they were served sweetbreads with Jerusalem artichokes, brown veal sauce, and slivered black truffles. From that day forward, Newton was in love with a tuber.

He begged to meet the creator of the dish and was introduced to Chef Lacombe. They talked for half an hour. Unfortunately, Chef Lacombe spoke only French, so Newton's peppering of questions about truffles went mostly unanswered. But he was pleased when the Chef said, *"Vous êtes un jeune homme selon mon coeur."*

We have the same heart.

Newton knew if there was anyone in the world who could get him truffles quickly, it was Chef Lacombe.

Newton's Essay About Truffles (written for *Literary Arts* 8, the previous year)

Many people think that truffles are chocolates that most often appear at Christmas. Those people are dumb. People who are slightly smarter will say something like, "Aren't truffles a type of mushroom?"

Intelligent people know that truffles (Family Tuberaceae, sub-division Ascomycotina: Tuber and other genera) are an underground fungus with a heavenly smell. The best type of truffle is the black truffle (Tuber melanosporum). People shouldn't be prejudiced against fungi.

Truffles grow in the soil beneath the drip lines of hazel and oak trees. They emit a steroid similar to the pheromone that male pigs produce. This is a brilliant plan, because when female pigs smell that truffle scent they go absolutely crazy. They have to have it. So they dig in the ground, believing they're about to experience a romantic encounter. Truffleurs train these pigs to find large stores of truffles.

The Babylonians, the Egyptians, the Greeks, and the Romans all bowed down before the flavour of the truffle. In the late nineteenth century two thousand tons of truffles were harvested. But two world wars ruined the land that the people required to tend their truffles. Oh, and killed a lot of the truffle-gathering peasants, too. Today only two hundred tons are harvested in France, which means truffles are now extremely rare and worth as much as four hundred dollars a pound.

In my humble opinion, truffles are worth every penny.

Une Porcine, Il Est Ordered

After studying propaganda in *Literature and Survival 9*, Newton hurried back to his room. He checked the weather on his laptop (no change), then phoned Chef Lacombe.

"*Bonjour.*"

Newton's brain usually froze when he had to speak French. "*Bon-bonjour. C'est Newton de Starker. Je désirer une porcine truffle pour mon* recipe, *vitement.*"

He was surprised at how well the words had flown out of his mouth.

"*Vous voulez commander un cochon qui fouille les truffes? Vous êtes certain?*"

"Am I certain? *Oui! Oui!*"

"*Combien est-ce que vous êtes prêt à payer?*" Chef Lacombe asked.

"How much? How much?" Newton said automatically. Then he came up with a number. "Umm. *Cinq cents.*"

Chef Lacombe sniffed. "*Peut-être.*"

Newton gave him the school address and after an enthusiastic "*Au revoir,*" he smiled broadly. He'd just ordered the perfect truffles. His smile faltered. He was pretty sure that's what he'd done, anyway.

What Happened in France

Chef Lacombe called his younger brother in Riez, France, and explained what he needed. His brother walked out of his stone house, got into his Citroen, sped past the four white columns outside of town, and turned left.

After several minutes and numerous turns he putted through the old wooden gate of a stone fence and into a farmyard that was older than the French Revolution. It looked as though it had been sacked several times. He got out of his car, stretched, and was met by his uncle, a farmer in his late sixties, clad in overalls, big boots, and nothing else. Not even a T-shirt. His grey, hairy chest was exposed to the world. They spoke in French and laughed in French, especially when the uncle heard how little money their new client was willing to offer. Several jokes about Americans passed between them.

The two meandered around the piggery. Litters of pigs were scattered here and there in the barn, some with black, rugged skin and thick, curly hair, others bright pink and bald. The farmer paused to reach down and pet giant sows that could have knocked over a bear. He whispered to them in soothing tones. Several raised their heads to have their chins tickled.

He stopped at a pig whose name was Madame Bovary. She was as high as his hip and was the great-great-granddaughter once removed of Audrette, Napoleon Bonaparte's truffle-hunting pig, the greatest pig ever to have hunted truffles. She shook her majestic hide and the black Rorschach spots danced over her haunches. Each indicated the shape of a truffle, or a map to some great and secret truffle trove. She held her chin straight and proud, granting the farmer the great privilege of scratching her head.

Then she stepped aside to reveal the runt of her litter—a tiny, iridescently pink pig. Light from the window dappled its skin, making it glow.

"Josephine," the farmer said.

The tiny piglet nodded to the farmer and followed him to the gate. She waited as he opened it, then trotted through it, towards the truffleur's car.

Now she would have a new life.

Excerpt from *The Survival Handbook of the Jerry Potts Academy*

When you are confronted by a survival challenge, the question you must first ask yourself is, "What would Jerry Potts do?" Would he give up hope, fall to his knees, and freeze to death in that blizzard? Or would he slice a hole in his horse's stomach, scoop out the viscera, crawl inside, and live to tell the tale? You will survive only if you are willing to go above and beyond the ordinary. Keep your knife and your wits sharp. Use every tool at your disposal.

Mercantile Fitness

After a lunch of ham sandwiches and coleslaw, Newton and Jacob rushed to their next class, *Mercantile Fitness and Survival 9*. The Academy buildings were in no way connected, so they were forced to go outside. It was all part of the Potts plan to invigorate the students' bodies and minds.

In the classroom Newton sat and carefully blew his nose into a handkerchief. He briefly examined the contents, then deposited it into the pouch on the inside of his sporran.

"I wonder what gory details we'll get today. Will we learn how to slay the mercantile dragon?" Jacob asked.

Newton shrugged. His eyes shot needles at Violet as she waltzed through the door, but she only ignored him.

Headmaster Dumont arrived and lumbered up to the front. He glared at the class until they all fell silent, then he thundered: "Outdoor class today, people. Bring your field journals."

Everyone jumped, checking to be sure their ebony *sgian dubhs* were in their sheathes on their lower right legs and patting in their backpacks for their field journals.

Newton had a little black one he'd bought from the camping section in the Canadian Tire store on Moose Jaw's

Main Street. The book had a latch, was waterproof, and could likely survive a nuclear detonation.

We look like ducklings, Newton thought as he and the class followed Dumont, single file. Newton searched the sky for lightning-bearing clouds. Only a few harmless puffs.

"Well," Jacob said, "this is an odd beginning."

"Maybe it's a *Lord of the Flies* thing," Miranda Jakes said. Her hair was a bright, impossible pink.

"Maybe," Jacob said. Miranda walked on and Jacob shouted after her, "Whoever holds the conch may speak!"

"What's that mean?" Newton asked.

"It's from the book. I'm sure she recognized it. She's a reader. She reads real books."

"Yep. Anyway, there doesn't seem to be an end to this march."

The class trudged a quarter of a mile along the banks of Thunder Creek. Finally, in front of a wall of bushes, Dumont paused and turned to them.

"The key to running a good business is being able to survive the competition. What you will learn here at the Jerry Potts Academy will serve you well in the business world and the natural world alike." He pointed his sausage-sized finger at them. Marcus Mitsou, a student from New Guinea, actually stepped back a bit in apparent fear. "Imagine being in a plane crash in the middle of the frozen tundra. Your duty is to haul yourself out of the wreckage and know exactly what to eat."

"The other passengers," Newton whispered, which got a laugh out of a few girls and Jacob.

Mr. Dumont gave him a glower that would have shrivelled a moose. "Mr. Starker, you of all people should take survival seriously."

Newton bristled. "I do."

But Mr. Dumont didn't seem to hear him. "Survival means setting aside some of the taboos and niceties of civilized society. In the instance of an airplane crash where there is no food available and no easy escape from the crash site, you may be forced to consume bits of those unlucky enough to have died. Flesh is protein. You need protein to survive. Eating human flesh, if that is all the protein available, is the logical thing to do." Mr. Dumont was big enough to consume several passengers for breakfast alone. "Of course, it is not right to *kill* someone in order to consume their protein. I assume you all learned that from ethics class already. It is not every man or woman for herself. We survive together.

"Today we are searching for herbaceous perennials. As you know from your studies, these are plants that appear to die off in winter, but their roots survive. They are often overlooked. They can be consumed on their own or be used to flavour soup. You've seen pictures of them in your handbook. So find some. Now!"

The class scattered, digging around in the riverbank and surrounding grassland like raccoons. Newton drove his *sgian dubh* into the soil again and again, nicking his hands twice. He managed to find a familiar fern plant, which he showed to Mr. Dumont, who said, "Eat the leaves."

"They taste yucky," Newton said.

"They'll put hair on your chest," Mr. Dumont said. "It's Pasture Brake. Don't eat too many of the leaves raw because the thiaminate enzyme will eliminate vitamin B from your body. Oh, and don't whine about the taste."

Whine? Newton thought. *I was observing.* Newton noted the plant in his field journal and dug on. A ledge of dirt fell into his hole and he breathed in a pocket of air that smelled like spring. Whatever had left that scent in the ground made his mind vibrate with visions of flowers.

He sniffed again and it was gone. There didn't appear to be any plants or seeds that could have released the scent. But his brain felt a little more awake. The experience reminded him of truffle pigs and how they could locate the scent of truffles.

"You forget to wear deodorant?"

Newton recognized Violet's nasal voice. He turned to her. She had dirt on her hands, a smile on her face.

"No, why?"

"You keep sniffing the air like something stinks. Maybe it's just your own natural aroma."

"Are you suggesting I stink?"

She shrugged. "If the smell fits."

A passage from the *Survival Handbook* floated to the top of his mind: *When confronted by a shark, shout in the water. If it continues towards you, then strike at its gills, that's the most sensitive area of a shark.*

Newton assumed Violet's gills were hidden under her hair.

"Don't you have someone else to bother?" he asked. "Someone of your own kind? A jackal, perhaps?"

She smiled, but there was a thin line of sadness in it. She opened her mouth, closed it, and strode on.

A Few Points about Moose Jaw

It was a city of 32,123 inhabitants built on the Moose Jaw River and was a retirement and tourist zone. Many members of the British royal family stopped in Moose Jaw on their way to somewhere else. They always left thinking, "How quaint." Oddly enough, the 1930s gangster Al Capone was said to have muttered those same words on his first visit to the city. However, between them he placed a swear word.

Some believed that the city's name came from the Native American word *moosoochapiskanissippi*, which means "the river shaped like the jaw of a moose." Others conjectured that the name originated in a local legend about a pioneer who mended his wagon wheel with a moose's jaw. Still other historians thought the city's name was based on the Cree word *moosegaw*, which means "warm breezes." In the winter, Moose Jaw was often warmer than the nearby communities.

No one really knew for sure how the city was named, which was exactly the confusion experienced in Newton's hometown of Snohomish. The name, also that of a local tribe, seemed to have come from the Native word *sdoh-doh-hoh-bsh*, which could mean one of three things: "lowland people" or "sleeping waters" or "a style of union among them of the braves." Newton decided that the confusion explained why so many in both towns drove so slowly; they were never quite sure where they were.

The city's main tourist attraction was the Tunnels of Moose Jaw. Gaggles of travellers arrived by bus, train, and car to explore the tunnels under the city built by bootleggers and Chinese immigrants. These were rumoured to have been the home-away-from-home for Al Capone many years ago. Thus, every second restaurant or bar featured the Capone name in some way. The tunnels, a spa, and a casino were the vibrant commercial heart, lungs, and spleen of Moose Jaw.

Newton's favourite thing about Moose Jaw was that it was in the light-blue zone of lightning strikes. The red and the yellow zones were the worst zones in North America. Snohomish was in the grey zone, just a titch safer than Moose Jaw. The white zone received little to no lightning, but taking advantage of that would mean living in Greenland or Antarctica.

Of course, where Newton was concerned, one lightning strike was one too many.

An Illuminating Visit to
the Grand Matron of the Starker Family

On Saturday afternoon, Newton walked along the path through the Highland Courtyard. He was on his way to visit his great-grandmother, Enid Evelyn Starker. Though he hadn't seen her in over four years, he remembered her clearly. The night before, his dad had badgered him again: "Be sure to visit Enid." Newton would rather have been strapped to a stretching rack.

Before his mother's death, his family had visited every two years. His great-grandmother had moved to Moose Jaw in the 1930s to marry a lightning-rod salesman. They lived in a house that had over five hundred lightning rods on the roof. Newton had seen pictures of it. The lightning that struck the rods would be diffused down several cables into the ground.

A breeze carried the smell of fresh horse manure. The eleventh-graders were at the stables forking hay and dung into the back of a large truck. *If they can survive that, they can survive anything.* Newton wasn't looking forward to his grade's turn on manure duty. *At least it'll be in the winter. Maybe it won't smell so bad.*

After his first few days at school his arms were sore from swinging axes, shovelling, and sawing branches. His legs ached from hiking, riding horses, and mountain-biking. Walking would be the most he could make his body do today.

It was a half-hour trudge to the nursing home, but it was sunny with no chance of rain. He'd checked the weather seven times before he left. There were plenty of buildings he could dash into for shelter if things changed. Under a tree was the worst place you could be (that was rule number eight). Though lightning usually hit the tallest object in its path, sometimes it didn't. If he was anywhere outside he could still be blasted into tiny pieces by a partial blow.

Several Moose Javians stared openly at Newton. *Must be the kilt.* It was like a police uniform; everyone knew at first glance that he was a student at Jerry Potts. Unless, of course, they were staring because he was Lightning Boy. *Stop it! Stop it!* he shouted in his head.

The Welakwa Home for the Elderly boasted a meticulously manicured lawn that a golfer would drool over. The sidewalks were wide, the bay windows large. Old people in wheelchairs watched him through the windows, some like eager puppies, others like suspicious bulldogs.

Newton was surprised to feel a twinge of jealousy. They had survived to old age. His mother hadn't. *It's not fair.* He wanted to punch out the sky.

He signed in at the front desk and made his way down the hall. The floors shone like mirrors and smelled of lemon. At his great-grandmother's room he knocked on the door. A scratchy voice shouted, "Come in if you have food, other-wise go away."

He walked in. Great-grandmother Starker was in her wheelchair about ten feet from the window, staring outside. Her white hair glowed in the sunlight.

Newton cleared his throat and she turned her head slightly. Her wizened eyes wrinkled up a little more when she saw him. "Oh, you," she said. "Your father sent a letter to warn me that you'd be coming." Her eyes—one blue, one grey—burned holes through him. He wanted to flee. He sensed she was a force of nature—a typhoon or a landslide—that ought to be avoided. *Toughen up, Newt. You're in survival school, for heaven's sake.* He made himself cross the room.

"Why are you here?" she asked.

"I came for a visit. I plan to visit every week."

"Oh joy." She glared out the window again.

"I can come back," he said. "Perhaps another time would be better . . ."

"No. You've dragged yourself here and despoiled my room. Sit down." Her stick-arm gestured from beneath her shawl. She'd painted her fingernails black.

Newton was about to lower himself onto the ottoman when she erupted, "Not there! Sit on the wooden chair. It's more easily wiped."

Blushing, he sat on the chair and faced his great-grand-mother. She was hard to look at—it would have taken a team of morticians hours to count every folded wrinkle.

"Tell me about your pointless life," she commanded.

"Uh, I'm doing well in school."

"That's not an accomplishment. You're a Starker. We're smarter than other people. It's all that extra electrical activity. Surely you've done something else worth mentioning."

Newton shrugged. "Not really."

"Then what's the point of breathing? Die now and make more room for the rest of the world."

Newton ground his teeth. "So what have you done that's so great?"

She coughed out a chuckle. "I survived."

She was right. There was no better accomplishment for a Starker. "How? How did you do it?"

"I don't give up my secrets so easily, boy. You'll have to earn them."

He nodded. Another test. "Well then, would you at least tell me why you think the lightning strikes us?"

A sly smile cracked Great-grandmother Starker's lips. "I'm sure your mom told you all about the first documented Starker to be hit? Andrew Starker. Born in 1745. Ha. I've read his journals; he was smart, and completely mad by the time he got fried. He believed it was because he'd stolen taffy from a shop in Philadelphia when he was a kid. For some reason that haunted the weakling."

"Is that what you believe?"

"What I believe? I've heard all the suppositions. Is it a curse? Who would curse generations of families? Is it in our blood? *Pffft*, sounds like hogwash. Is it God? Is it the Devil?

Such deities wouldn't waste their time with us." She snickered. "I'll tell you what I believe."

Newton leaned closer.

"I think we are angels, Newton."

"What?" Great-grandmother Starker was the furthest thing from an angel that he could imagine.

"You seem shocked. I'm not talking about movie angels. I mean the Eternal Fighters, creatures in the Bible who were above mankind, who wielded swords and conquered lands. And the Powers That Be—God, if you will, or maybe Odin or Zeus, who knows—are trying to wipe us angels from this planet out of jealousy."

"But . . ." Newton paused.

"But what, Newton?"

"That's not logical."

With that, his great-grandmother cackled long and hard. "We are beyond logic, Newton. Haven't you figured that out yet?"

Newton was silent.

"You seem pensive, Great-grandson. Perhaps I've blown your mind."

Newton didn't know what to say. His great-grandmother had been born in 1906. Maybe back then people were raised to believe in ghosts and angels and demons.

"The more you think, the more I'm bored," she said. "I've seen it all before. Everything. So entertain me. Now!"

"I still don't understand why this happens to us."

"Oh, here!" She wrapped her bony fingers around her wheels and rolled to the bookshelf, grabbed a book, and tossed it to him.

Newton caught it. It was ancient, and pieces of the cover flaked away like scales. "What is it?"

"It's the journal of your septuply-great-grandfather. He was a whiner just like you."

He opened it and gently flipped the pages, yellow with age.

"Thank you!" he said. "Thank you."

Several Short Excerpts from the Journal

Newton marched double-time back to his room at the Academy with the book wrapped in newspapers in his backpack to prevent it from being banged around. Sitting on his cot, he unwrapped it carefully. His brain was vibrating with the possibility of discovering the source of the Starker problem. He read the first entry.

July 9th, 1769
I, Andrew Bullden Starker, do begin this journal in the twenty-fifth year of my life. It shall verily be a collection of my thoughts, reminiscences, ruminations, and observations about the natural world and the nature of all things and shall be read and marvelled at by many generations henceforth to come.

Newton smiled at his ancestor's pomposity. Perhaps it was just the way people wrote in the old days. He turned the pages, slowly, each one threatening to disintegrate at his touch. He stopped five pages in.

It was with such rapidity of thought that I brought my unencumbered mind to bear on the task ahead. With clarity, and to the obvious surprise of my guests, all slow-witted by comparison, I said, "Forty-five draught horses." There was a gasp. They were no doubt shocked at my display of brilliance. They chattered amongst themselves like monkeys.

Newton was now sure that Andrew had the greatest ego of the eighteenth century. The next three pages were stuck together, so he skipped them and read some more.

September 28th, 1777

Yesterday I carried the bell from the Old Pine Street Church in my wagon, my intention being to hide it in the straw at my farm. We do not want the Red Coats to melt it down and, in turn, fire our bell back at us. To me, at least, it seems probable that the enemy will easily control the city for some time to come. Perhaps one day citizens will forget that the bell exists and I may be free to sell it myself, piece by piece. It is a precious metal, made more so by this conflagration.

As I was crossing my neighbour's field the sky grew cloudy and the moisture on my forehead and my personal moisture under my shirt increased tenfold. Suddenly, a jagged bolt of lightning struck the earth next to the wagon. The horses were severely agitated. I felt a rush of fear and even exhilaration. A second bolt landed in front of the horses and then it seemed to me no accident. Surely, it was intended for me.

I considered the proximity of the bell; the possibility of it being the attraction. Or perhaps the heavens had overheard my thoughts regarding the sale of it. No matter the cause, the weight of the bell was now a liability, preventing us from speeding away from the storm. I therefore decided to force the bell off the back of the wagon. I halted. At the rear of the wagon I placed my hands on the bell and at that very same moment a bolt of lightning struck me.

Me. It did not strike the bell. The heavens had aimed at me. My mind slowed down and I felt the electric energy enter the top of my skull, the heat eliminating each and every thought.

For one luminous moment, I saw three glowing figures.

Newton scratched his head, wondering if that many electrical volts could conjure up imaginary phantoms. He read on.

The figures appeared to be constructed of St. Elmo's Fire, looking up at me from the side of the wagon. They moved in such a way as to suggest a desire to communicate. Finally one spoke, but hoarsely, unintelligibly. The electrical current left my hands and entered the bell with a great flash. It began ringing, softly. It cracked, and the figures vanished.

For many moments I could not breathe. I heard the bell ring and I felt as though I were a child again. I remembered stealing taffy from the corner shop on Montgomery Street, the first sinful action of my life. Given my recent

wayward thoughts, perhaps the lightning was a punish-
ment. Or a warning.

To my great consternation I could not let go of the bell.
Three hours later a surprised farmer and his men came
and, with much pulling and grunting, unstuck me and
took me to their humble home. No matter how much I
washed, I could not rid my hands of the coppery hue of
the bell.

And the figures, the entities, populate my imagination,
burned there.

Newton reread the last few paragraphs, searching again
for any sign of logic, a reason for the lightning to have hit
Andrew Starker. Newton skipped several pages ahead and
found another entry in ragged handwriting.

My children, my beautiful children, are dead. They
have been struck down by the heavens. Now I can only
pray that lightning will come for me as well.

Newton turned to the last entry, dated June 17, 1792.

We have been blessed with one last child. My son,
Benjamin. All the rest lost to lightning over the years. We
shall not let him go out of doors. His will be a life of books
and games.

The lightning will come for me soon, I feel it in my bones.

I have calculated figures, I have looked for the logical answers, and I have written many epistles to my relatives and have studied their replies. I have unearthed our relatives in Scotland, the MacStarkers.

And now I understand, my father came to this land not to escape the poverty. He came to avoid what I can only call "The Electric Blight." And he did, as he died of cholera. Lucky man!

My father's father was struck by lightning and killed, so too his father—it is beyond reason. A curse. The widows write back with family legends that tell of ancient ancestors going back hundreds of years dying by a blow from the heavens.

Newton rubbed his head. *So it has been happening for eons.* The thought chilled him. Yet, there was a glimmer of hope. After all, Andrew had survived that first strike. And his great-grandmother was still here. And Newton himself.

I cannot understand our curse. Are we too vain, we Starkers? Like Achilles, raised and dipped in our own vanity? And now the heavens punish us? When I stole that taffy it was vanity. I believed it belonged to me because I was Andrew Starker. I deserved to have it. It is because we love no one more than ourselves.

Is it our name? We have Norse blood in our veins, and in the Norse tongue sterkr means strong. Were we strong?

Or strongly cursed? Generation after generation has died at the whim of the gods. Perhaps they simply intend to blot us from the earth.

I know it will come for me. I see it when I close my eyes. In nightmares. I know it lurks above, those hungry tongues of electricity.

When will it end?

And that was it. Some twenty blank pages followed.

Newton skimmed the last entry again. So, he had Viking blood in his veins! He had always suspected there was something heroic. But still . . . why were they plagued with lightning?

His septuply-great-grandfather had gone mad trying to find the answer.

That won't happen to me! Never! I won't let it.

As he went to close the book, writing on the inside of the back cover caught his eye. The embellishments on the letters made him think it was a woman's penmanship.

Andrew Bullden Starker was murdered by lightning on July 14th, 1792. He was a good father and a good husband. He shall be missed.

Newton's Rules for Survival

9) If your hair stands on end, you are about to be struck by lightning. Begin evasive manoeuvres.
10) Lightning travels down telephone wires. Use only cordless phones.
11) Airplanes are safe. Their bodies are aluminum, which is a good conductor of electricity. The lightning flows along the skin and shoots back out into the air.
12) Even if you can't see any clouds, they may lurk just beyond the horizon. You are still in danger, as anvil lightning strikes horizontally away from the parent thunderstorm.
13) Check the weather. Re-check the weather. Check it again.

A Tragic Greek Hero in the Flesh

At Jerry Potts, Sunday morning was a day of contemplation and work. Newton skimmed through Andrew Starker's journal again, hoping the answer would leap out at him. Why did it have to be such a puzzle?

A knock at the door startled him out of his thoughts. He got up and opened it. "Just on my way to the mess," Jacob said, cheerfully. "Want to tag along?"

"Sure." Though Jacob had sat with him during several meals, it was the first time he'd dropped by beforehand. Once again he questioned his mother's "no friends" policy. Surely it would be okay to have a friend so long as there wasn't any lightning around.

As they walked across the courtyard Jacob began explaining his new novel, which had something to do with spirits from beyond that pulled an unsuspecting character into their fantastical realm.

As he spoke, Newton daydreamed about the upcoming Outdoor Expedition. Would there be bears? Wolves? Skunks? No matter. He would build the best lodgepole lean-to, the grandest deadfall trap. By the time he was done with the outdoors, it'd be like living in a five-star hotel. He'd get the highest mark and be remembered forever in the Hall of Heroes.

"Does your connection with lightning worry you?" Jacob asked.

"What?" Newton's happy dreams popped like a balloon.

"Well, to be honest, I Googled your name. I read about all your relatives who've died from lightning strikes. I'm very sorry for your losses."

Newton blinked. "Uh, well, thank you."

"It got me thinking about Greek mythology. You're a classic tragic hero, cursed by the gods."

"Uh, I guess. Maybe." Newton had read about Zeus, the lightning god, wondering if somehow there was a connection between old myths and the way lightning used the Starkers for target practice, but he'd found no Greek bloodline in his family tree. He tried to smile. "If I'm a classic hero, you can be my classic sidekick."

"Cool, I always wanted to be an Argonaut. Anyway, I just wanted you to know how I was suddenly struck by the . . . the tragedy of your situation. Other students think it's kind of funny."

"Which other students?" Newton spat out. "Tell me." Then he took a deep breath. *Rule number six. Don't get angry. Count to ten. One . . . two . . . three . . .*

Jacob backed off a bit and pushed up his glasses. "Oh, don't worry about them. They're barbarians. What I was trying to say is it's not a laughing matter. These lightning strikes are real. You must find it all very frightening, and maybe frustrating. Is that how it feels?"

No one had ever asked him how he felt about the lightning (other than a psychiatrist at the University of Washington who was doing a thesis—she'd been cold as a dead fish).

"I—I, uh, yes. It's frustrating. Very frustrating. But it gives me something to think about."

Jacob laughed, and Newton felt an overwhelming sense of warmth. Of . . . buddiness. *So this is what friendship is. What a good feeling.*

"Can I ask a few more questions?"

"Yeah."

"Well then, how have you stayed safe all these years?"

"My mother marked the start and end of lightning season on the calendar, so I knew when it would be okay to go outdoors. And our TV was always set to the weather channel, and when there was a storm we'd just stay safely inside the dome."

"Dome?"

"Oh, I grew up in a monolithic concrete dome. My father designed it. It's virtually weatherproof. Tornado-proof. Lightning-proof, too, of course."

"You never played outside?"

"Just in the wintertime. The swings sure froze my butt in January." He laughed, and Jacob nodded, smiling.

They walked through the Hall of Heroes and Newton glanced at the plaque. Beyond it was the board where their marks were due to be posted the following day.

They ventured into the mess, where a swarm of people surrounded them. The air smelled like burnt toast, and Newton felt unusually warm and strangely at peace with the world. He'd shared some of his story and Jacob hadn't laughed at him.

"I'd like to read your new book," he told Jacob.

"Really?"

"Of course."

"Did you get a chance to read some of *The Brilliad?*"

"Uh, well . . ."

"Be honest."

"I struggled a bit, but I think that's because it was so deep."

Jacob grinned from ear to ear. Newton was amazed: all it took was a few kind words to make him beam like that. "I'll print you a copy before the end of the day."

Newton cleared his throat and they walked on.

"Thank you, for asking about the lightning," he said. "I really don't get to—"

The next thing he knew he was horizontal. He'd put his hands out just in time to keep his face from smacking into the floor. Violet was looming over him.

"Be careful," she said.

"You tripped me."

"Don't be absurd, Rod."

"Rod!" Newton crawled to his feet, seething. "Why do you keep calling me that?"

"Figure it out. You're the brilliant one." She turned away.

Newton glared at her back, his mind clicking. *Rod. Iron. Metal. Lightning.*

He clenched a fist. "You're calling me a lightning rod!"

Several students laughed.

His neurons were firing like an atomic chain reaction. Messages skipped, shot, careened, and bounced from one synapse to another. Angry messages became a chorus of voices all shouting for his attention. *Newton! Newton! Over here! I'm angry! No, I'm angrier!* He thought of all the times he'd been teased. Of his mother's death. Newton felt as if his brain would explode and splatter across the room.

He sucked in a deep breath.

The Second-Stupidest Words Ever Spoken by a Starker

"Violet Quon!" Newton's voice knifed through the chatter and shuffling feet. The crowd of students parted, revealing Violet. "You are . . . atrocious!"

Violet grinned. "Please. I was only teasing. Take a chill-pill, Rod."

"A chill-pill?" Newton inhaled through his nostrils and spoke the second-stupidest words ever spoken through the last twenty generations of the Starker family (the stupidest being when Andrew Starker ran towards a summer storm, clutching a lightning rod and shouting, "Give it your best shot, you spawns of the Devil!" They did. He died.). "Violet!" Newton growled. "I, Newton Goddard Starker, challenge you to a duel. I must defend my honour. Your choice of conflict. Chess! Fencing! Racquetball!"

"Boxing," Violet replied without missing a beat. She looked coolly at her own fist. "Unless, of course, that's too manly for you."

"Boxing it is! Perfect! I'm ready. Bring it on!"

Newton had never boxed. Nor had he ever fought a girl.

Jacob tapped him on the shoulder and Newton spun around, his panther-like reflexes on red alert.

"Calm down, Newton. Is this wise?"

"Yes," Newton hissed. "There's a time for thought and a time for action. I'm done with thinking!"

A sea of kilts, bow ties, and acne-clouded faces crept closer. The students formed a square around Violet and Newton. Two pairs of red boxing gloves were pulled from a locker and passed from hand to hand.

Violet slipped the gloves on and began a warm-up dance, her ghillie brogues clicking on the hardwood floor. Newton jammed his hands into the oversized mitts and tried to tie the laces, but the thumbs were too bulky to allow a good grip. *Boxing is easy,* he told himself. *Connect your fist to your opponent's body. Simple as that.* Newton bit the lace, pulled, and unravelled his knot. A seed of doubt sprouted in his mind. *What am I doing? Giving in to the Starker anger.* He struggled to tie a new knot. *I'm about to fight a girl, for crying out loud.*

"Here!" Jacob tied the gloves, grimacing at the saliva sticking to his fingers. "Newton," he whispered.

"Don't try to talk me out of this. I mean it. Just don't!"

"If you back out now you'll look like a chicken. Of course, if you win you will have just beaten up a girl—a Pyrrhic victory!"

"A what?"

"You win but you lose. You know, like King Pyrrhus's victory over the Romans, where he won the battle but lost the . . . Look, I'm just saying Violet's strategy is doubly clever. Either way you lose, so you might as well try for victory. This is how to win." Jacob leaned in. "You've got to eat lightning and crap thunder."

Newton shuddered. Why mention lightning at a time like this?

"It's a line from *Rocky*," Jacob said. "I've always liked it. Here's my real advice: Hide behind your gloves."

"Hide? I'm not going to hide!"

"After the first few blows to the head you'll understand. Look at the confidence in her eyes, she's a pugilist at heart. I hear her dad's a Mountie, probably trained her since birth. Wait till she tires and maybe you'll get lucky with a hay-maker. Oh, and beware, she's a southpaw."

Newton should have asked what a southpaw was, but instead he nodded, inhaled, and set his jaw. "Prepare to defend yourself, Violet. You won't make fun of me ever again. Never ever—"

"Put up your dukes," Violet interrupted. "You can finish your speech from the floor."

He raised his gloves. The combatants circled like two kilted pit bulls. She jabbed with her right and he shifted, avoiding the blow. "Ha!"

He danced around her, at one point slowing down to do a deliberate, modified foxtrot. Violet stared with a furrowed brow. She swung with her right again, this time brushing his forehead. "Ha!" Newton said, but not so confidently this time. She was proving to be fast. She could knock out a few teeth.

"My grandma hits harder than that!" Jacob yelled from the crowd.

Newton's mind wrestled with the situation. *How can I knock her out without hitting her?* It was a Zen riddle. He didn't want to punch her in the chest; that would be creepy. If he hit her nose he might break it. She did have a nice nose. *Stop thinking about her nose. Stop.* What if she started to cry? He decided her jaw would be the most logical target. He'd thump her lightly, just enough to scare her into surrender.

"Don't call me Rod again!" he shouted, and swung his right fist.

Violet's left fist was a red comet, and in the microsecond it took to connect squarely, one thought resonated between his ears: *Southpaw means left-handed.*

The Mysterious Event that Occurred

Newton flew backwards, arms flapping, birdlike. Kilts rippled, sporrans rattled as students leaped out of the way. His head struck the rib of a radiator. Lights sparked across his mind's eye and pain cha-chaed up and down his spine. He shuddered as his field of vision went black.

Newt. Newt. Newt.

His mother's voice. She was a human neon sign glowing blue, her hair a frazzle of electric light.

Am I dying?

She reached out and spoke tenderly, her voice crackling like a transistor radio. *My darling Newt. You've got to try harder. Count to ten. Get better marks. Embrace your destiny. And don't forget to brush your teeth. I love you.*

Then darkness blotted her out.

What the Other Students Saw

Newton flew headfirst towards the radiator. Some students covered their eyes; others squinched them together and grimaced. A few wondered: Would he break his neck? Would his skull crack like an egg? What colour would his brains be?

They were disappointed. Newton's skull remained intact.

It was Jacob who pushed his way to Newton's side and shouted, "Someone call Nurse Garchinzki. Now!"

Twenty cellphones were pulled out. Nineteen of the students called friends, telling them, "You gotta see this!"

Violet was the only one to call the nurse.

The Awkward Awakening

Light shot into Newton's eyes. He stared at the sun, his best friend. He loved the sun. He would have hugged it if his arms had been long enough and it weren't twenty-seven million degrees Fahrenheit.

He blinked until it became clear that the light was too small to be the sun. And it was surrounded by a tiled ceiling.

His brain ached as though someone had been playing basketball with it. *Ouch. OUCH.*

He turned his head slowly and the room came into focus. A small, arrow-slit window with the blind drawn. On the bedside table, a pitcher of ice water and a rose in a half-filled drinking glass. On the wall, two large words painted in red: "Get Well."

So, he was in the Academy's Aid Station, lying on an army cot. Somewhere, nearby, lurking like a giant spider, was Nurse Garchinzki.

What happened? Then his jaw throbbed and everything came back: his fancy footwork, the evil fist of Violet, that moment of weightlessness before he hit the floor.

I lost. I lost to a girl. Shame turned his guts to lead. He could never go back to his classes. There wasn't a cave deep and dark enough to hide in.

An overpowering loneliness hit him like a truck. *Why isn't Mom here?* He felt as though he had just seen her. He blinked too late to stop a tear. *Why am I crying?* He tried to lift his hand to wipe his eyes but his arm flopped across his stomach like a dead fish. *I can't cry. I don't have time. I have to plot my revenge.*

The door opened and his heart leaped. He strained, forcing his hand up to wipe his face.

Nurse Garchinzki chugged across the room like a bulldozer.

"My head hurts," he said.

"I nursed men in Bosnia with holes in head. They didn't whine half as much as you. You are stupid, stupid boy."

Newton's eyes widened. "Me?"

"Yes, you. Get in fight with girl. Hit head. Now I must wake you every hour to be certain there is no damage on the brain."

"I—I am not stupid!"

"I do not argue with stupid boys. I shall wake you every hour."

She was as good as her word. All morning, on the hour, she tapped his forehead with a wooden spoon until he opened his eyes. Then she would ask: "What is three plus two?" The first time she cracked him with the spoon until he spat out the answer. He began shouting out "Five" the moment he heard the creak of the door.

He yearned for the gentle song his mother used to sing:
"Good morning merry sunshine, how did you wake so soon?
You scared away the lightning-bearing cumulonimbus clouds
and shone away the moon."

Newton's Mom

Sometimes when Newton remembered his mother's death he thought of lobster. Baked, stuffed lobster that he'd made once as a treat for his parents.

As they were eating in their dome his mother had suddenly grabbed Newton's arm and hissed, "There has to be a reason. It's like we were chosen." She'd waved a lobster shell in her other hand, scattering bits of lobster and stuffing across the table. Newton stared in horror at the crazed look on her face and the way she was treating his creation.

"There *is* a reason, Newt! I think I now understand. We're being shot into a new realm. Yes, that's what the lightning does. I know it! I know it! I know it!"

Newton and his dad gawked at her.

The following day she was laid out on the couch, a cold washcloth across her forehead. "It tires you out," she confessed, "the waiting. The knowing that one day you'll be struck down. I don't know how Great-grandma has lasted so long. But you can survive, too, Newt. Don't give up the fight. Promise me!"

"I promise, Mom."

The circumstances surrounding her ultimate encounter with lightning a few days later were shrouded in mystery.

Newton's father fetched him from school. His face was pale, his eyes red. Trembling, he embraced Newton. "Son, I have bad news. Your mother . . . Mom died an hour ago. She was struck by lightning near the Presbyterian church. She didn't suffer."

Later, when he thought about it, Newton couldn't figure out why she'd been there. It was the first day of lightning season; they had it clearly marked on their calendar. She shouldn't have been outside that day.

Her funeral would be burned into his memory forever. Snohomishians, curious strangers, and paparazzi gathered to watch her casket as it was carried out of the church. They looked like monkeys to Newton.

As he watched the pallbearers lower his mother's coffin into the earth, he shook with anger. The gawkers didn't have a clue about what it was like to be a Starker. He focused on the flowers strewn across the top of the casket. Camera flashes lit up the petals. Each flash reminded him of how his mother had died.

What *The National Globe* Wrote

Lightning Strikes Twice!

Here's a shocker! Delilah Starker from Snohomish, WA, was struck by lightning for the second time in her life and killed. Her father, her brother, and other members of her family have died in the same manner. It appears this Starker family is cursed. Delilah Starker is survived by her husband and her son, who, it is said, lives in the basement of their dome-shaped home and never sees the light of day.

On a Cellular Level

Newton's cellphone played a muffled version of *Ride of the Valkyries*. His eyes opened like lazy clamshells. His arms were slugs that inched towards his phone on the dresser. Once again he was surprised by the rose. What was it doing in a drinking glass?

He clutched his phone, brought it to his ear.

"Mom?" he whispered.

"Mom?" a familiar voice echoed. "Newton, is that you?"

"Yes." He couldn't remember who owned the voice.

"Why are you asking for Mom?"

"Dad? Dad! Why—why are you calling?"

"Why? Because I was told you've been injured. What happened? Are you okay?"

"I'm fine. I'll be released soon."

"Well that's good, at least. I've been wondering if I should have sent you so far away."

"It's a great school, Dad. I like it here."

"Well, apparently you don't like all the students. Headmaster Dumont told me you were in an altercation."

"It wasn't an altercation. It was a tussle."

"A tussle put you in a sickbed?"

Newton held his head. "Well, there were fisticuffs, too. But she deserved it."

"She?"

"Violet."

"You fought with a girl?"

"I . . ." Newton couldn't think how to explain it. The whole thing did seem pretty doltish.

"Did you count to ten beforehand?"

"No."

His father cleared his throat. "Well, what was the tussle all about?"

"She . . . uh . . . I think she's jealous of me, Dad."

"Jealous? What's going on, Newton? Fighting isn't like you."

"She made fun of me in front of everyone."

"Ah. I know how . . . sensitive you are."

"I'm not sensitive!"

"Then why'd you get so angry?"

"Testosterone, Dad."

Silence. Then, "Ah, yes, of course. Testosterone." He almost sounded proud. "But Newton, you've got to control yourself. I've been thinking that maybe I could fly up there for a few days. I could be there as early as this evening."

Newton wanted to say, "Yes." It would be so good to see him. Why had he come to this school, anyway, so far from his bedroom in their dome? The safest place on earth.

"Newton?"

Newton let out a long breath. "No. No. I'm okay, Dad. I know how busy you are with work."

"You're more important, son. I'd come in a heartbeat. Do you need me?"

"Thanks, Dad. Really. I'm fine. It's only a bump."

His father laughed, that friendly chuckle Newton loved. "I still can't believe you fought a girl. A *girl*." He paused. "And you lost. How's your male pride holding up? She must be big."

"She's Godzilla-big."

"Well, you're sounding like your old self, at least. If you need anything, call. Especially if you want to talk. Any time, you know you can do that, right?"

"Yes, Dad. Of course."

"I miss you, Newton. Take care now. And—count to ten!"

Doing His Best Lazarus Impression

At eight o'clock on Monday morning, Nurse Garchinzki woke Newton by tapping on his forehead. He shot up, and coming face to face with her, recoiled with a gasp.

"You are free like bird now," she said. "Fly, fly. But eat breakfast first." She pointed at a tray.

She turned to go, then stopped in the doorway. "Oh, and you are commanded to visit Headmaster Dumont."

Dumont? Newton groaned.

Newton took off his green hospital gown. How he'd gotten into it was a mystery. He decided to remain in denial about the obvious: Nurse Garchinzki had dressed him.

He fumbled his kilt on and staggered to the window to survey the Academy grounds. It was a castle, really, considering the long stone walls, the brick belfry, and the turrets. He stared up at the sky. Not a cloud.

Outside, the first person he ran into was Jacob, cutting across the Highland Yard.

"Newton! This is great tidings! You've arisen from the dead, like Lazarus."

"Yeah. Up and at 'em. So to speak."

Jacob patted Newton's shoulder and got a shock. "Ow!"

He gritted his teeth, then shook his head and tried to grin. The concern in his eyes was magnified tenfold by his glasses. "I tried to visit, but Garchinzki went all Cerberus on me."

"She did what?"

"Guarded the door like the dog that guards Hades. You know, three heads, a lot of slobber. Anyway, I couldn't get by her. You look like you've been hit by the black plague. Are you sure you're supposed to be walking around?"

"Of course!" Newton breathed in, hoping more oxygen would bring the colour back to his face. "I'm fine. Just a little out of it."

"Well, you've certainly created a stir. People are talking."

"Oh? What are they saying?"

"The fight has already reached legendary status. Some believe it lasted eight rounds. Others say you peed your kilt."

"Peed my kilt?"

Jacob shrugged. "Well, you know how rumours get started. The good news is that your time in sick bay means you won't be in so much trouble. Brilliant planning on your part! Letting Violet knock you out was the best thing you could've done."

"Violet didn't knock me out! The radiator did."

"Oh, sorry. That's what I meant."

Newton's head throbbed. An electrical charge shot from the tip of his left big toe to the top of his scalp.

"Newton? You okay?"

"Fine. Has anything happened to Violet?"

"Dumont is reportedly fuming about the fight. Violet might even be expelled."

"Ha!"

"Be careful what you wish for. He'd have to expel you, too. It's the law of equal punishment." Jacob squinted through his glasses. "You've learned your lesson from all this, right?"

"Yes. Next time I won't choose boxing."

"No! Just ignore her. She's not worth your time."

"Ignore her? Good strategy, Jacob. That'll get on her nerves." Newton paused. "Uh . . ."

"Uh, what?"

"Did my kilt, like, was it decent?"

"You mean did your underwear show?"

"Yes."

"You were covered up perfectly."

Newton sighed. "Good."

Jacob pushed his glasses back up his nose. "Gotta go. I have to get over to Thunder Creek for an extra credit outdoor survival class. Maybe we'll learn more about the constellations, like which one's the Swan and which is the Bear. Or we'll dig up roots, boil bark, and disguise ourselves as ground squirrels." Jacob paused. "That was a joke."

"Oh, I get it," Newton said. He slapped a knee. "Have fun."

Newton walked past the belfry and followed the sidewalk around the courtyard, passing several ninth-graders who stared at him. Some giggled.

On the stone steps of the administration building, he

96

needed to use the handrail to climb up. At the top it occurred to him that he couldn't remember walking the fifty yards across the courtyard. *Maybe I should have stayed in bed.*

He looked back to where he'd come from and saw Violet lurking beside the statue of Jerry Potts, watching him. *Like a coyote watching a lamb. She'll soon see that I'm a wolf in sheep's clothing.*

Newton sent her a withering wolf glare, but after a second he realized it was just Maggie Surtis, a girl from Alaska.

He struggled to open the heavy oak door. Again, time snapped forward. Now Newton was at the end of a long hall. The distant sun shone through tall windows, lighting several paintings of wheat fields. He blinked. *I have to concentrate. One step at a time.*

He shuffled to the office and stopped to adjust his kilt. Then he looked up at a life-sized painting of Jerry Potts. The tracker was testing the wind with his finger, dressed in leather clothes, a derby hat, and tassels along his arms and around his knees. The master survivor.

That's something we have in common.

Newton saluted Jerry and reported in. Miss Humphreys, the secretary, looked up. "Oh my, are you all right, Mr. Starker?"

"I'm . . . okay," he replied. "I had to convince Nurse Garchinzki to let me go, but I just couldn't miss a full day."

"You poor, poor boy," she said. "You are so dedicated. Mr. Dumont will be pleased. He asked you be sent in the moment you arrived."

Newton tottered over to the headmaster's office. Before he could knock, a voice behind the door said, "Come in."

Headmaster Dumont stood next to his desk, dressed in a green lumberjack shirt and a kilt. "So. You're *not* dead."

"Oh no, sir, I'm very much alive. I do have a headache, though. I shouldn't be given any homework. Nurse Garchinzki's orders."

He'd been hoping to get a smile out of Dumont. Instead, the headmaster's eyes grew stony.

"Nurse Garchinzki had a slightly different opinion when she reported on your condition this morning. She felt the strap was in order. Lucky for you, Mr. Starker, we're not allowed to use it any more." Dumont crossed his arms. "Well, I won't lecture you about boxing in the dorm—you're intelligent enough to know better. Nor am I interested in the reasons for your fight; they're always the same: ego and poor judgment."

Newton's eyes widened. "I don't have poor judgment!"

"Lacing up against Violet was unwise. She's trained in several martial arts."

Newton shook his head. How could he have known that? She'd cheated by training so much.

"So, Mr. Starker, how do you suggest I punish you?" Dumont asked.

"Nurse Garchinzki was punishment enough."

That, Newton was relieved to see, got a slight smile.

"Newton, we thought long and hard before allowing you into our Academy. I read the scientific papers about the

Starkers and lightning. Having you here meant spending thousands of extra dollars on safety equipment. Even with it, your presence puts everyone here at an elevated risk. Every student, every instructor. The risk is manageable, and the board felt, aside from wanting to help you, that it would be good for the whole school to learn more about surviving lightning strikes. We do not turn away those in need of survival education. But you must work with us."

Newton hadn't given a thought to all the money spent on his account. Or the fact that they could just as easily have said no. *I let them down by fighting.* For a few moments he considered the impact of his mistake, but his remorse was soon wiped out by thoughts of Violet: *She made fun of me. Me!*

Dumont waited patiently for an answer.

"I will work with you, sir," Newton finally promised. "I won't let you or the board down. From this moment on, I will be your best student."

"It's not about being best," Dumont said. "It's about learning your limits. You chose to disobey Academy rules. Rules are what keep this Academy strong. I will give you another choice, though. Would you prefer an intellectual punishment or a physical one?"

A trap! He couldn't imagine what either of the punishments would mean. He whispered, "Physical."

"Fine. You have KP duty. Kitchen Police. You will report to Mess Master Tawrell every morning, noon and evening. She will assign you work."

Newton pictured carrot peels, boiled cabbages, and overcooked noodles. The smell of burnt toast and porridge. Dumont must have remembered Newton's school application essay about his love of fine food. There could be no worse punishment. "But . . ."

"Welcome to the real world, where there are consequences for your actions. We expect *healthy* competition among our students, but we also demand co-operation. Remember that."

"But . . . but . . ."

"You are dismissed. I suggest you hit the books. They won't hit back." Dumont didn't smile at his own joke.

As he left the office Newton's head throbbed.

From: headmasterdumont@jerrypottsacademy.com

Date: Monday, September 3

Subject: Marks/Culinary Dish/Punishments

To: alladdresses

Dear Students,

If you are reading this you have survived your first week at the Jerry Potts Academy. Congratulations. We have posted your marks in the mess hall, and will continue to post them every Monday morning. This is to foster healthy competition among classmates. As many of you know, whoever has the highest marks in each grade at the end of the year will have his or her name engraved on a bronze plaque in the Hall of Heroes.

The following are messages of importance:

1) Mr. McBain reminds grade nine students that your main dish will be created tomorrow in Culinary Arts class. Be prepared to cook.
2) Edison Nuttle, a senior, has broken his leg after falling off a horse. He will be recuperating in the nurses'

station. Visitors are welcome from 3:30 to 5:00 p.m. Edison gets extra marks for setting his own leg.

3) Our bell-ringer this week will be grade nine student Violet Quon. Violet was involved in fisticuffs. She has also been assigned stable duty. Newton Starker, the other participant in the incident, has been assigned KP duty.

4) The first quarter Outdoor Expedition will begin on September 18. That is two weeks from now. I remind you: visualize success. Sharpen your minds.

Enjoy your week. Work together, learn together, survive together.

Sincerely,
Mr. Dumont, Headmaster

P.S. I have reprimanded several students who have been dressing in a slovenly manner. This will not be tolerated. Demerit points will be handed out. Remember, the staff at the Jerry Potts Academy see everything.

Une Delivery *L'*Unexpected

Newton laughed after reading the e-mail from Dumont. "Yes! Yes! Yes!" Violet would be punished. Bell-ringing and stable duty. *Ha! She deserves every stinking moment of it.*

His glee sent a sharp spark of pain through his skull. He threw his legs over the edge of his cot and pressed his palms to his temples. It felt as though someone had hammered a spike into the top of his head.

Kitchen duty! The thought of it made his guts churn, and for a nanosecond he wondered if Violet had been given the better deal. He wouldn't even get to cook. He'd be cleaning up guck—not so different from shovelling manure.

Newton traced the events that had led to this. Violet had tripped him. She had called him "Rod." Then the Starker anger had taken over. *I have got to keep my cool. I have to hold this Starker's ship together.*

His cellphone burst into symphonic song.

"Hello?"

"May I speak to Newton Starker?" a woman asked.

"Speaking."

"This is STC Parcel Express. You have a parcel here for pickup at the bus depot."

"I do? What's in it?"

"We aren't allowed to look inside packages, sir."

"Oh, okay. I'll be right there."

Newton checked the weather (sunny and 20 degrees Celsius, 68 degrees Fahrenheit), locked up his laptop in the ammunition box, and hid the key in his right running shoe in his closet. His mood lifted when he remembered the order he'd placed. *My truffles are here! Tomorrow, the whole class will be amazed by my recipe. That ought to make up for this boxing fiasco.*

He grabbed his bike helmet and went first to the armoury, where he stood in the Hall of Heroes staring at the printout of students' marks. Since there had been only three days of classes, he had received marks for a short in-class essay about creating tools from stones, wood, and vines: 87 percent. Two points behind Violet. *Ha! Call me, Rod, will you? I'll surpass you yet.*

Her name would never be in the Hall of Heroes. His would.

At free time, he went to the Physical Education office and signed out a bike. He pedalled towards the heart of Moose Jaw. After five minutes his legs were rubber and the ache in his head was almost unbearable. But he needed those truffles.

Newton locked up his bike just off Main Street at the Moose Jaw bus station. The woman at the counter wore a tag with "Mandy, Pleased to Meet You" written across it. She didn't seem pleased to meet him. She plopped a pet cage down on the counter. It was solid plastic with several air holes. "There you go, bub." *Bub?*

"It's a pet cage," Newton said. Mandy was flipping through invoices. She didn't lift her eyes.

How odd. He touched the cage as though he were about to defuse a bomb. Suddenly something inside moved, and Newton jumped. For a moment he suspected he might be on a reality TV show. Would it be a rabid dog? A skunk? Or was it his head injury conjuring up a bizarre event?

He slowly unlatched the door, opened it a crack, and peered inside.

Two intelligent eyes blinked back at him. A clean, perfumy smell emerged.

Newton opened the door a little more. The eyes were set in a hairless head, centred by a round and perfectly pink nose.

"It's a pig," Newton blurted. Mandy went on flipping her invoices.

He squinted at it. It was the same size as a small poodle. It appeared completely calm, as though it were meditating. Its eyes did follow Newton's movements. Attached to the door was an envelope and a little jar.

He opened the envelope and found a note: *Voici vos truffes et votre truie. Elle s'appelle Josephine.*

Newton shook his head. My pig? Josephine?

Oh no!

Chef Lacombe hadn't understood his French! The tiny jar was labelled *Les Truffes du Fermier Lacombe, en vente au grand rabais.* Truffles! At least something had worked out. Now he could make his recipe as planned.

He looked down at Josephine. She seemed quite happy to see him and nuzzled his hand when he reached inside.

"Hey there," he said. "What am I going to do with you?"

She oinked. It was a friendly sound.

He closed the door, threw his vest over her cage, and carried her out to his bike. It took several attempts to balance the cage on his handlebars. On his way back to the Academy he stopped briefly at the Co-op grocery store and bought the other ingredients for his recipe. He passed a few Moose Javians, but no one looked too closely at the pet cage.

When he got to his dorm, he sneaked Josephine up the back stairs and into his room. He set the cage down and opened the door. She took a few steps out and sniffed around.

"Good pig, good girl." Was that how you talked to a pig?

She let out a quiet oink and two grunts.

Hmm. How to keep her from dirtying the floor?

He brought her a Thermos cup of water. She'd need food. In his life he'd only eaten pigs (several recipes came to mind) and had never concerned himself with what *they* ate. More importantly, could they be house-trained? He decided to look online.

Now, where's that key? He checked under the cactus in his window. Not there. Looked behind the picture of his mother. No sign of it.

The pig followed him closely as he paced around the room. She seemed to be grinning, as though they were playing a game. Newton stuck his head under the cot. She poked her head in next to his.

"What are you doing?" someone asked.

Newton banged his head on the bed frame so hard he saw stars. "Jacob," he said, looking around for the pig, "You really should knock."

"The door was open. I thought you'd swooned from your head trauma and fallen on the floor."

"Only girls swoon. Guys black out."

"True enough."

Newton looked down just in time to see the pig's tail disappear under the bed. With any luck she'd stay there. "I'm trying to find the key to the ammunition box. I hid it somewhere."

The pig poked her head out from under the bed and raised an eyebrow at Jacob, then oinked.

He did a double-take, removed his glasses, looked at the lenses, put them back on, and stared at Josephine. "There's a pig in your room!"

"So there is." A sudden stab of fear struck Newton's chest. Jacob could report this to the floor sergeant. "Look, there's been a mix-up with the truffle company. They sent the pig by mistake. Now I have to find my key so I can unlock my laptop and figure out what to feed her and whether or not she's house-trained. I've checked all over, so help me find the key, okay?"

"You forgot the magic word."

Newton sighed. "Please."

The closet door slid open and the two boys jumped.

Somehow the pig had pushed the door open and run

inside. There was a bang and a bump, and she charged out with Newton's running shoe and dropped it at his feet like a dog. With her right front trotter she flipped it over, and the key landed on the floor.

Newton stared in awe at the pig. "Did you see that?"

"Yes, she found the key. That's remarkable!"

Newton knelt down and scratched the little pig's head. She nuzzled against his hand. "You're amazing, Josephine," he whispered.

"Are you missing anything else?" Jacob asked. "We should test this."

"Please, Josephine, find my stash of illicit magazines."

She cocked one eyebrow, zipped under the cot, and a moment later was pushing out a short stack of magazines.

Jacob grabbed the top one, which featured several scantily clad women on the cover posing provocatively with computers. "*MacAddict?* That's your illicit magazine? Newton—"

"This is spectacular! She is a four-legged miracle!" Newton leaned over and whispered, desperately, "Josephine, please find a way for me to never get hit by lightning."

She stared up at Newton, tapping one foot. Morse code? *Tap-TAP-tap-tap*. He listened for a message, forgetting for a moment that he didn't know Morse code. She sat on her haunches, made a *harrumph* sound, and scratched behind her right ear with her hind leg. Was she trying to tell him something?

"Pretty please?" he added.

"Might as well ask her to create world peace," Jacob scoffed.

"It was worth a try," Newton said, picking her up tenderly. He set her on the bed, where she lay down. He stroked her head and she grunted, opened one eye, then closed it. He patted her back until she snored softly.

"Hey, I don't believe it!" he said, looking at his hand and then at Josephine.

"Don't believe what?"

"I haven't given her a shock, yet." He touched her again, gently. She didn't stir. "I've never been able to touch pets. Cats would get zapped so hard all their hair would stand on end. Dogs, too. Once, I accidentally killed a parakeet! That put a damper on my birthday party."

"Yikes! That is curious."

He rubbed his feet back and forth quickly on the throw carpet and touched Jacob's arm, producing a spark that sputtered like a firecracker.

"Ow!" Jacob jumped away from him, holding his arm and grimacing. "Stay away from me!"

"Sorry. I just had to see if it was me or the pig. How very interesting."

Newton unlocked his ammunition box and pulled out his shining white MacBook.

"I came to bring tidings," Jacob said, still standing several feet away from Newton. "I wanted to let you know first. Well, after my parents, that is."

Newton was busy Googling information about pigs. "Hey, all I need is a litter box. Cool. They *can* be house-trained. Bizarre."

"Did you hear me, Newton? I have tidings."

"Oh, what?"

"A publisher in Toronto wants my book. They called this morning."

"Oh," Newton said. A green tentacle of envy suddenly squeezed his heart. Jacob would be mentioned in the paper. He'd become famous. They might even put his picture in the Hall of Heroes. "Wow."

Josephine let out a series of oinks. And if he hadn't known better he would have said she was scolding him. If she actually was scolding him, then what for? Okay. So he was being a poor friend. He should be pleased for Jacob, not jealous.

"That's wonderful news. Absolutely wonderful." Newton shook Jacob's hand and this time, no shock. "This will be perfect. You'll get good credentials as a writer, some notice, then you can write my life story."

Jacob frowned. "Your life story? Uh . . ."

"I was kidding. I'm really pleased for you." And he was, now that he thought about it. Jacob had been working hard on his books. And he had talent. Besides, authors were on the lowest rung of the fame ladder. Newton just hoped that this new book wasn't one long sentence. "I do have a question for you, though."

"Which is?"

"What do you know about feeding pigs?"

Newton's First Taste of KP Duty

These are the things he did:

1) He scraped burned and dried scalloped potatoes from the casseroles.
2) He carried pails of slop—carrot peels, potato peels, onion bits, half-rotted melons—out to the compost station across the yard.
3) He attempted to have a conversation about recipes with Mess Master Tawrell, but all that came out of her hulking, no-necked frame were the words: "I hate that fancy stuff."
4) He scavenged old salad, carrots, and potato peels for Josephine.
5) He held his throbbing head. If there was any place more horrid than the Jerry Potts kitchen, he couldn't imagine it.

Newton Starker's Truffle X Quiche

8 ounces cooked X (this can be any meat, shaved,
   though salmon is preferred)

2 cups shredded mozzarella cheese (don't buy generic
   mozza!)

1 teaspoon chopped green onion (peel off the rubbery
   layer or you'll get gross bits in your mouth)

1 tablespoon all-purpose flour

½ teaspoon salt

2 ounces truffles, grated (black truffles, of course, from
   France—not Italy and NOT China)

3 eggs

1 cup whole milk

pinch nutmeg (not two pinches!)

9-inch pastry shell (deep)

Combine cheese, onion, flour, and salt. Carefully spread half
of mixture on the bottom of the pastry shell. Top with X.
Spread the remainder of the cheese mixture on X.

Put truffles, eggs, nutmeg, and milk in a blender on low
speed. Pour this liquid mixture over the ingredients in the
pastry shell.

Bake for 15 minutes at 450° F. Reduce heat to 350° and bake for 30 minutes or until well browned.

Serves 6.

The Secret Ingredient

On Tuesday morning when Newton heard the bell he smiled with great satisfaction. Violet was out there yanking on the rope and shivering. Ha!

He dressed quickly, threw the ingredients he needed into his backpack, and left Josephine with the command, "Don't make a mess." She shot an oink at him and glared as though deeply offended.

"Sorry, sorry," Newton said, raising his hands. Somehow, it seemed entirely natural to apologize to a pig.

He'd placed newspapers in a low box in the closet where she would, with any luck, do her thing. He left her fresh water in a dish on the floor. Next to it, another dish contained the scavenged food.

His first class of the day was *Culinary Arts and Survival 9* and he rushed into the room. *Today I'm going to set the world on fire with my cooking!* He wanted to shout that, but he knew the others would think he was odd. He carefully pulled the dry ingredients out of his backpack. The remainder he took from the classroom fridge. Everything was fresh.

"Yo, my illustrious bro!" Jacob said, and Newton couldn't help but smile. A *bro*. A brother.

A dark, familiar thought slithered into his mind. He'd

never had a brother. He often suspected it was due to the lightning problem, that his parents couldn't face the stress of protecting a second child.

Jacob was staring at him, waiting for a response.

"Yo, illustrious bro, back at you," Newton said.

"You okay?" Jacob whispered. "You popped away for a second."

"Popped away?"

"Yeah, zoned out."

"Oh, well, oh, I'm perfectly zoned now. Channelling my inner chef. That's what I'm doing."

"I'm making a gumbo stew," Jacob said. "Figure then it doesn't matter what the surprise meat is."

"Very good idea." Newton rubbed his hands together. "Bring on the culinary countdown."

Mr. McBain blustered into class like a five-foot-six summer storm.

"Heave ho, everyone! Top o' the morning and all that jazz." He was holding a large, grey plastic bag. "I suppose you lads and lassies are wondering what the mysterious main ingredient of your dishes is! Well, gather round." Newton could see lumps in the bag. A few appeared to move. Mr. McBain dumped the contents onto the great centre table and an immediate "*Ewwww*" rippled through the group.

Rodents. Dead, thankfully, but still with their pelts on, glazed eyeballs gleaming.

"May I introduce sixteen fine, plump specimens of Richardson's ground squirrel," Mr. McBain said. "Gophers, as the locals like to call 'em. Your new best friends. They live in vast multitudes across the prairie and there's one for each of you here today. They're going to be delicious!" He paused. "You're only as sharp as your knife, remember that!"

Within a minute Newton was at his station with an extremely sharp penknife in hand, holding his breath. He made a small incision across the stomach of a recently defrosted Richardson's ground squirrel. He was absolutely and totally disgusted, and looking around, he was clearly not alone in that revulsion.

Despite wearing rubber medical gloves, the sensations were still icky enough to roil the contents of his stomach.

"This frail vessel once held life," Jacob whispered from the prep station next to Newton's. He pushed up his glasses and positioned his penknife on the ground squirrel's chest. "Forgive my trespasses."

"It gets better after the first cut," Newton said. "Not much, though."

Newton made the incision longer.

"Do *not*, I repeat, do *not* cut into the internal organs!" Mr. McBain shouted from the far side of the room.

Despite the revolting task of preparing the gopher, Newton's mind was absorbed by the quiche recipe. *If the meat is gamy I'll have to wham it with the tenderizer hammer.*

"Careful with those guts, son!" Mr. McBain bellowed down Newton's neck, causing him to nearly drop his knife. The instructor moved around the room like a panther. "Now, all of you, insert your thumbs into the incision and pull outwards! The skin'll come away easily. You'll see!" He pointed at the class for emphasis with the middle finger of his right hand. (His index finger was missing. Rumour had it he'd left it somewhere in India.) Newton pulled. As promised, the skin fell away.

I only just got out of the sickbed yesterday, Newton wanted to shout.

"Ach, that's it, lads and lassies! We're cooking with petrol now."

Newton glanced at Jacob, who looked squeamish.

"You okay?" he asked.

"I'm fine, but this'll be the worst gumbo ever," Jacob said. Just then the gopher's innards spilled out of the incision. "I. Need. Air."

Mr. McBain gave Jacob a tap on the shoulder. "Lad, don't forget the eyeballs," he said, and Jacob fled, just in time to throw up in the hallway. The sound of it made Newton want to do the same. He gritted his teeth. He wished he could go help Jacob, but didn't want to take the chance of losing marks. A moment later the janitor arrived, mop and pail in hand. Soon Miranda and two others ran to the hallway and used the pail as well. When they were done, the janitor led the three of them away.

Newton's resolve got him through the gutting of the gopher, peeling back the membrane that covered the chest cavity and pulling out the heart, lungs, and windpipe. Soon he had all the remaining parts in a small pot boiling away on a bunsen burner.

"Boiling'll kill most anything that'll kill you," Mr. McBain announced.

I hope so. He shredded the mozzarella cheese, chopped the green onion, and mixed the two with flour and salt. He spread it across the pastry shell he'd made the night before. At the last moment he opened the jar of truffles so they'd be as fresh as possible. The scent made his eyes roll back. *That's what Heaven smells like.* He plucked out a truffle and closed the lid. He sliced the truffle thinly, all the while grieving its future lying next to gopher meat.

Soon, he was waiting while the quiche baked.

"Did you like the rose?"

He turned to find Violet standing there, her face guarded. She was holding a dish that looked like some sort of stew.

"Rose?"

"At your bedside, in the sick bay."

"That was you?"

"Yes. You were KO'ed, so I didn't chat."

"*You* left me the rose?"

"You're sure quick. Yes. Of course. I thought it would be a nice touch. After all, Al Capone sent roses after the St. Valentine's Day Massacre."

An order flashed through Newton's mind: *Pull the quiche out of the oven and dump it on her now.* But rather than follow it, he said, "I gave the rose to Nurse Garchinzki. She ate it."

For an instant, Violet looked as though she was going to cry. Then she kicked him in the shin. "You moron!"

The Starker anger rose to the surface like the Loch Ness

Monster searching for sheep, but Newton fought it back down. Revenge: a dish best served cold, with gopher guts on the side.

Only later, when Mr. McBain was tasting his quiche, did Newton get satisfaction. "Truffles! Tender meat! Lad, this is the best gopher quiche in the history of Potts gopher recipes. Top marks!"

Newton shot a look at Violet. Actually, revenge was best served straight out of the oven.

Excerpt from *The Survival Handbook of the Jerry Potts Academy*

One must always ask oneself, "Is the eye half empty or half full?" Take it as your mantra. But what does it mean? The eyes of any large animal contain a certain amount of water. It may be necessary to drink it, especially if you are trapped in the desert and your camel has just died. Pluck out the eyes and suck out the liquid. Squeamishness is weakness. The eye is always half full.

A Second Illuminating Visit with Great-grandmother Starker

Saturday afternoon, Newton checked the weather on his MacBook. He was a little worried about how warm and humid it was for September in Saskatchewan. There was no prediction of thunderstorms online, just the comforting image of a smiling sun. Nonetheless, in the back of his head the constant and unnerving electrical buzz had been jacked up a notch.

He phoned Environment Canada.

"Is this Newton Starker?" the man asked.

"Yes."

"You're our most frequent caller. We appreciate your faith in our system. There is absolutely no chance of lightning today."

And so Newton set off for the Welakwa Home for the Elderly. When he'd walked three blocks he shrugged off his backpack, lowered it to the ground, and opened the flap. Josephine stepped out, sniffing the grass on a perfect lawn.

"How do you like the fresh air?" Newton asked.

"*Oink!*" She trotted alongside him, and a few Moose Javians gawked. Newton shouted in his head: *Haven't you ever seen a truffle pig before?*

When he got to the front desk Newton signed in, and since the woman didn't bother to look down and see Josephine, Newton didn't bother to mention her.

He went to his great-grandmother's suite and knocked. A bitter "Come in" pierced through the door.

She was in the same place by the window, wearing the same shawl, with the same blanket over her lap. A pot of tea sat on the tray next to her. She looked down at Josephine. "You've brought lunch."

Josephine let out a squeak, then barked at the old crone. At least, it sounded something like barking to Newton.

"Feisty little piece of bacon, isn't it?"

"She's my pet," he replied indignantly.

Josephine bark-oinked again, this time at Newton. "I mean, my friend."

"You have a pig for a friend? How far the Starkers have fallen. It's a good thing the line will end with you."

"It won't end with me. And Josephine is very special!"

She smiled. "Ha, got your dander up."

Newton took a deep breath and counted to five in his head. *Don't fall into her trap, Newton. Try to find the positive in this visit.* He sat on the wooden chair across from her. "Uh, how are things here?"

"Boring and stupid. Old Man Munroe died on Wednesday. He was eighty-two. A loudmouth. I told him I'd outlive him. We even bet on it. I won! Ha! Of course, I can't collect my two bits because he's dead. But still, I won."

Newton blinked in awe. *What a horrible bet to make.*

He put his hands on his knees, leaned in, and tried to find something in his great-grandmother that was similar to his mother or himself. Only the eyes. Grey and blue. Eyes that were currently examining him.

"Well, are we having a staring contest or what?" she chided.

"Uh, so, I read the journal."

"Oh really. And what did you make of Andrew's pitiful life?"

"Well. He gave up, didn't he? In the end. Just completely gave up."

She pulled her shawl tight around her shoulders. "It's not about right or wrong; it's about weak or strong. If you hope to live any longer than a mayfly, learn that lesson, at least."

"That's partly why I'm here. I want to know how you've managed to live so long."

She smiled, gargoyle-like, displaying crooked yellow teeth. "Ah, my secret. All the other Starkers have died so young. So tragically. But I've outlived them all. So what's my secret?"

"Yes."

"Well . . . you are the last of us. I suppose I should tell you, on the off chance you'll live long enough to sire children. Wouldn't want to have the line die out." She paused to sip from her teacup, then her palsied hand lowered it onto the side table. Newton's brain pulsed and he leaned in, ears at the ready. "I once believed I could just move away from the lightning so I went to Alaska, but the nightly chatter of the Northern Lights nearly drove me mad. So I moved here, married a second-rate lightning-rod salesman, and hoped for something that would keep me alive. I kept living. To thirty, then forty, and on my forty-fifth birthday, I discovered what was keeping me alive. Spite."

"Spite?"

"Spite, Great-grandson. Lovely, gorgeous, unyielding spite. I hate everyone—everyone I have ever met, every man, woman, and child who ever breathed air on this ugly planet. Oh, it was just a seed in my heart when I was a child, but the longer I lived the bigger it grew."

"You hate everyone?"

"Even you."

"That's terrible."

"That's survival. Oh, it's not that I don't have moments of feeling sorry for you or your mother or your grandfather. But I have made a stone of my heart and I have survived. Idiots made up jokes and laughed about my father when he was killed. The lightning hit his Model T in 1910. I survived that blast. I outlived the schoolchildren who called me names and taunted me, the newsmen who told half-truths, the teenagers who left me out of everything. They're all dead and I'm still here. I'll even outlive you, Newton." She pointed a crooked finger at him. "Would you like to bet on it?"

"No. Not at all." Newton wasn't sure he'd win, especially when he saw the slate in her eyes.

"Your great-grandfather thought he would bury me. I was his ticket to cash, my fame helping to sell all those lightning rods. But I buried him. Then your grandparents, your uncle, your mother." The madness in her eyes softened for a moment and she sighed. "She was such a sweet child. I did . . . I did sometimes hold out hope that Delilah would live longer. But your mother gave up."

"She did not give up!" Newton couldn't believe his ears.

"Well, she forgot about the weather, then."

"What do you know, you old bat?"

"Settle down there, whippersnapper!" She leaned back in her chair. "Well, well, well. You actually have some spite in you. Good. Good." She eyed him. "Maybe you will survive. Do you have any friends? I mean, besides Porky here."

Josephine didn't even oink at that. Instead, she yawned.

"Not that many," Newton admitted. He thought of Jacob. And, oddly enough, of Violet, then pushed her out of his mind.

"Dump them. They'll just drag you down. Life is a sinking ship and we're all fighting for one solitary lifesaver." Her twiggy fingers balled up into a fist and she shook it as though she were about to roll dice. "So, that's my secret. You must cultivate a healthy sense of spite, Great-grandson. Spite. And maybe you'll even outlive me. But I doubt it, since I'm the Angel of Spite itself."

Now she truly did look insane. *The Angel of Spite? Good grief!*

"Well, that's enough wisdom imparted for today. What time is it?" she asked.

Newton glanced at his watch. "Almost four-thirty."

"Ah, wheel me out to the verandah, then. I want to see the old men bowling. Some of them still have nice bums, you know."

Newton made a sour face. He didn't want to think about old people's bums. Ever.

He wheeled his great-grandmother down the hall, with Josephine trotting behind. Enid seemed amazingly light; it was as though there was nothing in the chair at all. Where doors were open, she peered into the rooms as they passed. The occupants glared back. He imagined that she had mocked all of them at one time or another.

"Not so fast," she said, "not so fast." He slowed down. She seemed to want to soak up the attention. She held her head and shoulders straight, like royalty. Newton expected her to begin waving at any second. They passed through the tea room and conversations stopped. White-haired ladies narrowed their eyes.

"I'm afraid they don't like me much here," she said. "They're jealous of my good looks. And the fact I've still got my own teeth!" She shouted that last bit. "My own teeth!" She clacked her dirty teeth together and laughed.

"Clear skies, my boy," she said as they approached the verandah. "Clear skies! It's a glorious day. Roll me right up there." She gestured with her withered hand. "And stop hitting so many bumps! I suppose you can't have a driver's licence yet. Let's hope you never get one."

He wheeled her up to a spot on the wide deck where they could look down on the lawn bowling green. Several men in white hats, white pants, and white shirts watched as another rolled a ball along the grass.

"Ah, the games are on." Enid rubbed her bony hands together, emitting a sound like sandpaper. "Do you want to wager on who'll win? I bet it's the guy with the bony butt."

She was working so hard to be unlikeable that Newton was stricken with an odd sense of pity. He took in her frail body. Spite seemed almost to be leaking from her frame, making her appear smaller and smaller.

"You're my great-grandmother," he whispered as he touched her shoulder.

She looked up at him, anger boiling in her eyes. "Why is your hand on my shoulder?"

"You're family," he replied.

She was silent for several moments. Then she placed her gnarled fingers on Newton's hand. They were like ice, but Newton didn't move. "Your mother was the only one who would touch me," she whispered.

Newton immediately felt the hairs on the back of his neck stand on end. At the same moment, out of the corner of his eye, he noticed that the western sky was clotted with clouds. The hairs on his arms shot up straight as saluting armies and his ears buzzed as though a swarm of bees were encircling him.

"Does it seem a little quiet?" Enid asked.

Get down! he thought he heard his mother's voice scream. His great-grandmother swung around and yelled, "Back, boy, get back!" as she shoved him so hard he let go of the wheelchair and fell back, landing half inside the verandah door.

At that moment Enid Starker was struck by a flash of light so bright that Newton's pupils shrank to pinpoints. The lightning sparked through her, out her body, and down the metallic frame of the wheelchair. It crackled along the back of the chair and the bolt arced over Newton's head, striking the doorframe. The electrical energy seemed to dance for a few microseconds, and Newton thought he heard a fuzzy, transistor-radio voice say, "*I told you to be careful.*"

Mom? Mom?

He lay on the carpet for several seconds, his eyes throbbing in time with his heartbeat. He ran his hand over his skull—his hair was sticking straight up, but there was no other damage.

Slowly he got to his feet, keeping his eyes on the sky. The clouds had vanished, almost magically, and the sun was shining again. His great-grandmother sat peacefully, her wrinkled face at rest, her eyes closed, her mouth shut, and her bonnet smoking. Clearly she was dead.

Josephine oinked quietly and rubbed against his leg.

From the bowling green came an odd pattering noise that Newton at first took for rain.

It was clapping. The old men had stopped their game and were looking up, applauding . . . what? The sky? The lightning? The spectacular death? Newton didn't know which.

He wheeled his great-grandmother back inside the home, away from them. But the old women had plugged up the hallway with their walkers and wheelchairs. They were applauding too, relieved smiles plastered on their faces.

What *The National Globe* Wrote about Great-grandmother Starker's Death

Woman, 102, Struck by Lightning!

Enid Starker of Moose Jaw, Saskatchewan, Canada, was in her wheelchair on the front deck of her senior citizens' home when a bolt of lightning appeared out of the blue and struck her dead. Starker, as many of our readers know, is the grand matron of the Starker family, famous for having been decimated by lightning. Enid Starker is predeceased by her daughter, granddaughter, grandson, and other relatives, all taken by lightning. She is survived by her great-grandson, Newton Starker, age fourteen. He has been known to wear a tinfoil hat in the hope of deflecting lightning.

Calculating the Odds

In his room, Newton sat on the bed, staring at the wall. Absent-mindedly, he patted Josephine's head. The ambulance had come to the Welakwa Home for the Elderly and taken his great-grandmother away. Its lights weren't flashing. He had phoned his father, who promised to catch the next flight.

"Sit in the tail end of the plane, Dad. In a crash it will most likely break off. Statistically, most plane crash survivors were seated at the rear."

"That's morbid, Newton."

"It's survival, Dad."

"So it is. I see they're teaching you well. I'll be there as soon as possible. I promise."

Newton was happy about that. Being so close to the light-ning, and therefore coming so close to death, had set his brain ticking. Newton couldn't stop it from working on a list:

Things that I wouldn't be able to accomplish if I'd been hit by lightning:

- *Finishing the year with the highest marks and being in the Hall of Heroes*

- *Creating new, wonderful recipes*
- *Reading Jacob's new book*
- *Having the last laugh on Violet*
- *Getting to know Josephine*
- *Being with Dad*
- *Growing up*

Newton paused to relive Great-grandmother's death: how she'd pushed him away, the hair-standing-on-end moment, the crack of the lightning, and the applause. All the applause. *Do you want people to be clapping at your death, Newton?* There really was something worse than people making fun of you.

Yes, she had pushed him out of harm's way. That was something. That she would do such a thing created a firestorm of conflicting emotions for Newton. On the one hand, he didn't feel an overwhelming sadness, as he had when his mom died. He would never miss his great-grandmother as he did his mother. On the other hand, Great-grandmother Starker was the meanest person he'd ever known, but at the very last second of her life she'd chosen to save his. It was all so confusing. One thing he knew for certain: He felt sorry for her. She deserved a natural death.

Then it hit him. He was now the last Starker alive on planet Earth. The weight of this responsibility hung heavily around his neck. At the same time he felt a certain relief. He had survived Enid. He could check that off his list of accomplishments, at least.

He reached out and scratched Josephine's back, then picked her up and held her close. She gave a pleasant "*Oink.*"

A knock on the door startled him out of his reverie. Through the door Jacob said, "It's me, Newton."

"Come in."

Jacob walked in and sat on the trunk. "How are you feeling?"

"Tired," Newton said. "Very tired."

"I'm not surprised." There was an awkward pause. "I don't know what to say, Newton. I'm sorry about your grandmother."

He replied with a shrug, "She was my great-grandmother. And it was inevitable."

"Does it have to be? There must be a way to avoid the lightning."

Newton raised an eyebrow. "I don't see one."

Josephine oinked several times, seeming to admonish him. *She's right. I'm a depressing bore.*

Newton looked Jacob in the eye. "But I guess I just have to keep trying to find an answer."

"That's the spirit," Jacob said.

Another knock on the door. "Newton? It's Mr. Dumont."

Newton shuffled Josephine, grunting out complaints, under the bed, then answered, "Please come in."

Headmaster Dumont opened the door and squeezed through the frame. Newton hadn't realized how small his room really was until Dumont was in it. He filled every space, his swinging elbows threatening to knock out the windows.

"Oh, hello Jacob. It's good of you to spend some time with Newton, especially under the circumstances." He looked at Newton. "Again, I am sorry about your great-grandmother's death. Though this is the way of life, it's still hard any time we lose a loved one."

"Thank you, sir," Newton said, wincing a little at the term.

"I understand that your father will arrive in the next few hours. I wanted to tell you that you're officially relieved of your kitchen duties and you have permission to miss classes while you and your father prepare for the funeral. Instructors will give you makeup classes and tests so you won't fall behind."

"That is very kind of you, Mr. Dumont."

"It is our policy. The mourning period is important, when we're not in the field. If you were in a survival situation there wouldn't be time to mourn, but in civilized society we must make the time. The passing of a life is a grave matter."

Newton wondered if he was trying to be funny, but if Mr. Dumont had noticed the pun, he wasn't showing it.

"I assume," Mr. Dumont continued, "that the manner of your relative's death might be especially upsetting to you. It's only natural. I promise that we will do our best to protect you from meeting the same end."

"I appreciate that, sir."

"Finally, it is only two weeks until the Expedition. I have discussed this with my colleagues and we'll allow you to miss it, if you are feeling unprepared, mentally speaking."

"Miss the Expedition?" Newton said.

"Yes."

"Sir, I—I want to participate!"

"Being alone in the forest isn't just about survival. It's about facing yourself and your demons."

"But sir—"

"You don't have to decide right now," Mr. Dumont went on. "I do worry, in all honesty, that we'll never be able to teach you enough about lightning. Mother Nature has more mysteries up her sleeve than we'll ever understand. We can only let her flow through us." He laughed. "I sound alarmingly New Agey. Is there anything else you need?"

"I am doing well, sir. Well enough, thank you."

"Take care of yourself, Newton." His voice actually sounded gentle for a change. He turned to go, and at that moment Josephine chose to let out an oink, clear as a bell.

Mr. Dumont spun around. "What was that?"

Both Newton and Jacob covered their mouths and said, simultaneously, "Excuse me, sir."

He stared at them. Several emotions flickered across his face, then he shrugged and lumbered out of the room.

It wasn't until after they heard him going down the stairs that Jacob and Newton began to giggle.

You Are Cordially Invited to the Funeral of Enid Evelyn Starker

The burial was four days later, attended by Newton, his father, Jacob, and the manager of the funeral home.

"Any final words?" the funeral director asked at the end of the short service.

"Farewell, Enid," Newton's father said to the casket. "You were one of a kind."

"Goodbye, Great-grandmother," Newton added. "I hope you're in a happier place. And thank you."

The director pressed a button and the casket was lowered into the ground. As they turned to leave, Newton spotted a photographer crouched behind a tree, snapping pictures.

"Just let it go, Newton," his father said, putting his arm around Newton's shoulders. He pulled him close.

Let it go? Several revenge scenarios went through Newton's mind, including giving the photographer the finger. He settled on thumbing his nose at the guy and then at the sky itself.

Proposing a Change in Venue

The day after the funeral, Newton hung out with his dad, touring around Moose Jaw. His father had been staying at the Temple Gardens Mineral Spa while arranging the funeral and looking after Enid Starker's estate. Not surprisingly, she had left all of her money to the Welakwa Home for the Elderly for a new lawn bowling green. The only stipulation was that they had to build a statue of her.

They had dinner at the spa's restaurant. Newton chose veal portofino, since nearly every other dish included bacon, ham, or pork. He wouldn't be able to face Josephine if he ate one of her cousins. The tiger prawns were surprisingly delicious, even though Moose Jaw was so far from the sea. The veal was only passable. *If only the chef had used some truffles.*

"Are you happy here?" his dad asked during dessert.

"I don't mind Moose Jaw. It's bigger than Snohomish. But I wouldn't want to live here forever."

"I mean at the Academy. Now that you've been here for a couple of weeks, do you think it'll be what you hoped for?"

"Yes," Newton said. "I think so. And I've made a few friends. Well, Jacob, anyway." Jacob was looking after Josephine for the day; only a friend would take care of your pig. "I like the headmaster. And the teachers."

"Your mom was always a bit touchy about you having friends, but I think that's great news. Still, I had a lot of time to think on the way here and I have a proposal."

"Which is?"

"I think perhaps you should be home-schooled."

"Home-schooled? By whom?"

"Well me, of course."

"But I just got here!"

"Yes, I know, but . . ." His father scratched the back of his head. For the first time Newton noticed a few grey hairs at his temples. "We hired a new salesman last month and two more engineers. I should be able to reduce my workload to afternoons and some evenings. I could teach you in the morning. The rest could be done by correspondence."

"Correspondence?"

"Your mother and I spoke about this several times. She insisted you needed a normal education, but now I wonder about the wisdom of that. I especially don't like the idea of you going on this Expedition you've been telling me about."

Newton sighed heavily. He did miss his dad. And his comfortable bed in the lightning-proof, thunderstorm-proof, tornado-proof dome. And he, too, worried about his safety on these Expeditions. Could Dumont and the other instructors protect him out in the natural world?

"I don't want to lose you, son. I worry about you being this far away. And this incident with your great-grandmother. It . . . it could have been you, Newton. I couldn't stand losing you and your mother, too."

His father's hands trembled as he reached for his coffee cup. Newton had never considered how hard his going away must have been for his dad. If his mother had stayed inside the dome she'd have been alive today.

"I—I don't know. I really don't. I'll think hard about it, Dad. I'll need a few days, if that's okay."

His father nodded. "I'll respect your choice, Newt. You've got a good head on your shoulders. I just want you to know the offer is there."

Newton patted his father's hand, noticing, happily, that there was no shock. "You're the best, Dad. You really are."

A Bad Hair Day

Newton was having problems with his hair. He stared into the hand mirror. He'd used several gobs of gel and now his hair looked like a helmet. Josephine watched from her pillow near the radiator, oinking as though offering advice.

"What? Were you a hairdresser in another life?"

"*Oink. Oink.*"

"Is that yes or no?"

"*Oink. Oink.*"

Even as Newton smiled, a storm cloud of dejection was settling over him. His father had gone home the day before, and Newton pictured him sitting alone at the kitchen table in their dome. If Newton were there, he'd cook him a great meal. That would be fun.

It was Saturday, the day he would normally have visited his great-grandmother. She had been dead for a week. He recalled her gleeful face as she spoke about spite and survival. She had lived so long, it was true, but in such a state of anger. Or had what he'd witnessed really been a state of madness?

"What do you think, Josephine?" Newton asked. "Did Great-grandmother's spite help her?"

Josephine lifted her head, concern on her brow, and oinked emphatically twice.

"Sure wish I could read your mind," Newton said. "Seems to me it'd be a hard thing to live with so much anger and seething inside."

Newton turned his thoughts to school, resolving to work harder and set his goals a little lower. For example, he would aim to be in the Hall of Heroes by the end of the year, not try to have the highest marks the whole semester. His truffle recipe had moved him ahead of Violet on the marks front, but he'd only begun attending classes again on Friday, after missing four days. She'd be ahead of him this coming week.

He thought again about his dad's offer; he could go home any time. All he had to do was phone and his dad would book the tickets. It'd be great to spend more time with his father, who always worked so hard. "I mean it, son," he'd said. "It'd be fun to learn together."

The truth was that Newton did feel more nervous now whenever he went outside. He found himself checking the weather every few minutes. This only contributed to his general malaise.

What would make him feel better would be to get away for a while and enjoy dinner out. He scooped up Josephine, hid her in his backpack, tightened his kilt, and walked downtown. He passed some of the houses and buildings his dad had pointed out as wonderful examples of fine architecture, older buildings built with dreams of some great destiny for the city.

Newton entered Nit's Thai Restaurant, his oasis from the

Jerry Potts mess. He set down his backpack and unzipped it. Josephine poked out her snout.

"I've always got you," he said, patting her.

He drank a Dr. Pepper and devoured eight pieces of Guy Satay, an appetizer of sliced chicken marinated in spiced coconut and broiled on a stick. It was served with peanut sauce and cucumber salad, a combination that made it taste a little like candy. Perfect.

Newton's entree, Tum Yum Goung, arrived: shrimp in a sour consommé. He could taste chili, lemon grass, and lime. To die for.

The meal put his mind at ease for a while. Life didn't seem so bad after all, lightning aside. He had a great school, a great dad, a new friend, and a special pig. And he was alive. He could overcome his problems.

A rustle alerted him to danger, but before he could react he felt a sudden pain in his side and someone shoving him along the bench of the booth, smashing Josephine against the wall. She let out a grunt. Newton scrambled to push her back into his bag, then turned to face his assailant.

Sitting next to him was Violet, her nose only a few inches from his forehead.

"Hey, Newton. Dining alone, I see." Her breath smelled like egg rolls.

There was something poking into his rib cage and he hoped it was her fingernail, not her *sgian dubh*.

"Vi-o-let." He wanted to sound sinister, but it was more like a tire deflating. It made her laugh.

142

"I came to talk, Starker."

"Talk? Ruin my dinner, maybe."

"I was sitting at the back and saw you come in. It seemed the perfect opportunity to call a truce."

"A truce?"

"Yes." She pulled her hand from his side and Newton thought he saw the flicker of something metal. Perhaps her watch. Perhaps not. She couldn't be trusted. "We could work as partners. Study together. Imagine how well we would do as a team. We'd both be in the Hall of Heroes."

Newton smiled coldly. If Violet wanted a truce then that was proof she was in a weakened state. Or she was lying and setting him up for a fall. Either way, now was his time to strike.

He turned to look her directly in the eye and deliver something witty. Her eyes met his, unwavering. Her breath smelled minty now. He suddenly wanted to grab her and kiss her, and the thought made his head spin and his gut do a somersault. *What's wrong with me? This is insane. Get a hold of yourself, Newton.*

"Never," he said triumphantly, even as he was beginning to hyperventilate. "Never. Not in a billion years."

Tears seemed to be forming at the edges of her eyes. What was she playing at?

"Why do you do it?" Newton demanded.

"Do what?"

"Get on my nerves? Bug me? Annoy me? Why don't you get a life?"

Her answer was to grab a chopstick and drive it straight at his chest. Newton blocked the blow and grabbed another chopstick with his other hand.

"You snot," she hissed. "You stuck-up snot! No wonder no one likes you."

"Ha! Call me a snot, will you?" he said, parrying two other attempts she made to poke him. "Well, snot I may be, but I've been fencing since I was five. Ha!"

She feinted for his eyes, but he deflected it. "Ho!" he said, then Violet jammed her thumb into his solar plexus. He couldn't breathe and dropped his chopstick.

"You started it," she spat.

"Me?"

"You spilled your porridge on me. On purpose!"

"But you—you made my kilt drop in front of everyone."

She blinked, looking absolutely confused. "I had nothing to do with that."

"Don't lie."

"I didn't! I laughed my head off, but I didn't throw the rock. It was Mr. McBain."

Newton thought back to the moment: the tap of the rock, a large pebble really, hitting his belt; how he turned as his kilt fell; seeing Violet laughing, Mr. McBain feigning innocence.

A lesson. That's what it had been. So Newton would never buckle his kilt improperly again.

"You didn't do it?" Newton said.

"No."

Just then Josephine oinked and Violet's eyes widened.

"Did you hear that?"

"What?" Newton looked around.

"*Oink! Oink! Oink!*" Josephine was poking his leg with her snout.

"Oh, that." Newton moved his arm and a pink snout protruded from his backpack. "It's Josephine," Newton huffed, "my pig."

Josephine oinked, looked at both of them for a few moments, then daintily walked over Newton's lap and onto Violet's.

"Is she clean?"

"Of course."

Josephine grunted and rubbed her head against Violet's stomach. "She's so cute. And she smells like perfume."

"Okay, Josephine," Newton said, "get back here."

Violet scratched the top of Josephine's head and the pig seemed to purr.

"Josephine!" Newton hissed. She shook her head as though she had fleas, then leaped across Newton's lap and wiggled into the backpack, emitting a loud, derisive, "*Oink!*"

"You can go now," Newton said to Violet.

"I'm waiting for you to apologize to me."

"I never apologize," he lied.

She slid out of the booth, put her hands on the table, and leaned over to him. "You *will* apologize, one way or another," she snarled. And with that, she strode out the front door.

Newton chuckled feebly, put his head down on the table, and counted as he banged it ten times.

In the Bowels of Moose Jaw

By the time Newton went to leave Nits it was pouring rain.
It pounded down and bounced off the parked cars on Main
Street. He stood, backpack on, nose pressed against the
window, cursing Environment Canada. This storm had not
been foretold on the website. *My weather sense has failed me,*
Newton thought.

Rule number fourteen shot through his mind: *During
a thunderstorm stay away from conductive materials.* His
memory flashed back to his childhood, when he'd watched
the world from inside the family's dome like some lab rat
trapped in a glass cage. His whole life had been like this—
staring out windows, checking the weather. And it had been
like this for every Starker who had ever walked the earth.

It occurred to him that he'd been gripping the metal door
fiercely. He shoved the door open and stepped out into the
rain. A clap of thunder shook the city. *You don't frighten
me. You don't! I'll walk all the way back to the Academy. Just
watch me!*

A muffled oink floated out of his backpack, but he ignored
it. He swaggered down the street, ignoring another thunder-
ous growl as it ripped through the sky. Zeus was banging
his drums like a madman. Then followed a flash so bright it

bleached all the colour from the buildings on Main Street and momentarily blinded Newton. He bumped into something hard, blinked, felt one of the old-fashioned street lamps that decorated the street. Being, of course, much taller than Newton, it would be an easy mark for a bolt of lightning. He gasped and yanked his hand away. Now he was soaking wet, right to his skin. *I'm the perfect conductor of electricity.*

Another roll of thunder rattled the world and disrupted any rational thought Newton had left: *Go! Run!* He skidded down the sidewalk, yanked open the first door he could see through the spots in his eyes, and threw himself inside.

The room was warm and stuffed with tourists. Behind a long, polished counter stood two women dressed in 1920s costumes: flapper-style calf-length dresses, cloche hats with feathers sweeping across their foreheads. Behind them a large sign read "Tunnels of Moose Jaw: Get your tickets here!"

The tunnels! Perfect! He pulled his wallet out of his sporran and joined the lineup.

"Good evening, ladies and gentleman. I'm Fanny!" one of the women shouted. She picked up an umbrella. "I'll be taking you across the street to begin our lovely underground adventure. It'll be the bee's knees and the cat's meow! Just follow me!"

Newton panicked. There was no way he'd risk going outside again. He noticed other tourists trundling up from a set of stairs in the centre of the room. When no one was looking he feigned interest in the memorabilia on the walls and casually inched his way to the stairwell. When it was clear, he leaped down the steps two at a time into a dimly lit hallway—a tunnel, he presumed, deep below ground. He scampered through it, expecting a tour guide to pop up any second to stop him.

Newton came to the entrance of a large room with walls of stone, where whisky barrels and crates of fake "hooch" were stacked. He hid behind several barrels and shivered in his wet clothes.

The lightning couldn't get at him here in the bowels of Moose Jaw. It was like being at home in the dome. Dark. Safe. He pulled Josephine from his backpack and hugged her.

"I'll never win this, Josephine," he whispered to her, verging on tears. "I'll never, ever, ever win. I'm staying here forever. Forever." He could live off scraps left by the staff, the tourists. Maybe there was a secret stash of sandwiches that Al Capone had forgotten in a wall safe. Or a violin case. He'd drink whatever was in the barrels. He'd become the Phantom of the Tunnels of Moose Jaw.

Josephine oinked wildly.

"Shhh," Newton said. "This is home now. No need to check the weather every ten seconds. I'm sure we'll find plenty to eat for both of us. Do you like insects? There's a spider. A juicy spider."

She oinked again.

He remembered his mother during lightning season. How she would stay in the dome for so many days in a row, a pale ghost, fading more with each passing day, a strange look in her eyes.

Newton heard the mumbling of a crowd traipsing down the tunnel towards him. As it grew closer he could hear the tour guide pretending to sound like a mobster. The tourists entered the room and the guide said something about the distilling process. Newton huddled with Josephine tight in his arms, trying to stay out of view, but the next thing he knew a small boy was peering around the barrel, eyes wide.

"Who's that? Is that Al Capone's son? He's wearing a skirt! Why's he got a pig?"

Newton grabbed his backpack and leaped up. The tourists were staring at him like he was a freak. The guide was pointing a fake Tommy gun at Newton.

A freak? I'm not a freak. And I won't become some freak, hiding like a loser. What is wrong with me?

He fled down the tunnel, clutching Josephine, and ran back up the stairs. It was the right thing to do. He couldn't live down there. And he couldn't go back to the dome. He would tell his father tomorrow. As attractive as the offer was, Newton had to find his way in the real world. The Expedition would be his first test. He charged past the ticket counter, where a couple of Al Capone look-alikes gawked at him, and flung open the front door.

The glorious sun shone down on him all the way home.

149

Newton's Rules for Survival

15) Take shelter when you can count one minute or less between lightning and thunder. The closer those two are, the closer you are to death.
16) Plan your evacuation in advance.
17) If you are in a group, spread out. You don't want the lightning to be conducted from person to person.
18) If in the forest, seek shelter under a thick growth of bushes.
19) Check the weather. Check it again.

From: headmasterdumont@jerrypottsacademy.com

Date: Monday, September 17

Subject: The Expedition

To: alladdresses

Dear Students,

On Tuesday (tomorrow) of this week we will be embarking on the first quarter Outdoor Expedition. The buses will leave from the east gate at exactly 8:15 a.m. This will give you time to have breakfast, which will be your last civilized meal for over 52 hours. Be completely packed, and remember: The less you take the better. Those with allergies, asthma, or other medical conditions must take their puffers, EpiPen, or other medications.

These are your destinations:

Grade Twelve: Banff National Park

Grade Eleven: The South Saskatchewan Sand Hills

Grade Ten: Lake Winnipeg

Grade Nine: Cypress Hills Interprovincial Park

The goal for each participant in each region will be to find the talisman. The talisman's actual shape, size, and form will be a surprise, but you will know it when you see it.

Visualize success.

Sincerely,
Mr. Dumont, Headmaster

Survival of the Fittest and Then Some

Newton did up his kilt, his jaw set like stone. He tested his *sgian dubh* against his thumb. It was perfectly sharp, like his mind. He imagined himself holding the talisman high above his head as his fellow students cheered.

Of course he didn't know what the talisman would be, but in his mind it was a sword. Or a large truffle. Either way, he was holding it. In the three days since his visit to the tunnels, his resolve to complete the Expedition had remained strong. This was something of a relief.

He slid the *sgian dubh* into its sock sheath. Survival of the fittest. Kill or be killed. *I will survive and overcome all obstacles.*

He visualized himself in the Hall of Heroes. He had caught up on his homework and was just one mark behind Violet. Winning the Expedition would put him so far ahead that she would never catch up.

He tightened his belt so that the buckle dug into his belly button. After a few seconds he loosened it. *Whew.*

His class would soon board the bus to be dropped off in a remote location in the Cypress Hills. There they would fend for themselves for forty-eight hours.

These are the things Newton put in his backpack:

- Waterproof matches—to start a fire
- 8-ounce stainless-steel Sierra cup for cooking and drinking
- Flint—in case the matches got wet
- Fish hooks and a line—to catch fish
- Compass—to find his position
- Medical kit—which contained several items, including: potassium permanganate to sterilize water and use as an antiseptic; surgical blades and butterfly sutures to hold the edges of wounds together (if worst came to worst he could use his fishing line for stitches)
- Long, insulated pants—to stay warm at night. (His kilt didn't seem to have been made for survival on frigid Saskatchewan nights.)

He had his hat, gloves, layers of shirts and a jacket, dry socks, his sleeping bag, and canteen. He surveyed the room. That was everything.

He picked Josephine up off the bed and gave her one last hug.

"You hold down the fort. I've left enough food to last until I'm back. I'll miss you."

Then, as he was patting her head, Newton got an absolutely brilliant idea.

A Few Facts About the Cypress Hills

The Cypress Hills are a collection of low, rolling hills in the southwest corner of Saskatchewan. They shrug up against the flat prairie that surrounds them. They were one of the few areas not completely covered by ice in the last ice age. Consequently, habitat is different from the flatland below. The weather is different, too.

Their name comes from early French-Canadian explorers who used the phrase *montagne de cyprès* to describe the hills. The phrase was a little misleading; cypress trees didn't grow there. But the name stuck all the same.

It was a great place to trade whisky and hunt wolves. Oh, and massacre Indians. That's what a pack of American wolfers did to a tribe of Assiniboine who happened to be hanging out there. This convinced the government to quickly send the Redcoats, also known as the North West Mounted Police, to patrol the hills. They were guided on their various treks by the ornery tracker Jerry Potts.

The wolfers were driven away. So were the wolves and the bears. But the coyotes still howl across the hills. Elk still bugle. Trout splash in the water. Seven hundred species of plants thrive in the area.

They were all just waiting to welcome the students of Jerry Potts.

The Fabulous Instructions

All fifty-two grade nine students of the Jerry Potts Academy gathered at the edge of a ravine in the Cypress Hills. They were laden down with their gear and sleepy from the three-hour bus ride. Looming above them in the distance was Bald Butte.

"I can't believe they're letting us loose," Jacob said. "Will the hills ever be the same again?"

Newton smiled. Jacob actually looked as though he'd become stronger in the last month. He was standing straight, even though his backpack was full.

"The Cypress Hills won't get the best of us," Newton boasted. "It's survival of the fittest, of course. Eat or be eaten. Now we'll see who finds the talisman."

"I've been wondering about that." Jacob scratched the back of his head. "Does that mean only one student will get full marks and the rest of us partial marks?"

Newton nodded. "It must. It's a one-way ticket to the Hall of Heroes."

"But it seems unlikely that—"

Mr. Dumont suddenly loomed in front of the two of them. He stared until Jacob backed up a few steps, as if he'd been confronted by a bear. "Uh, we'll finish this conversation later."

"How are you feeling, Newton?" Mr. Dumont asked.

"Really well, sir."

Mr. Dumont reached into a backpack, pulled out what looked like a walkie-talkie, and handed it to Newton, saying, "Everyone is getting one of these. I'll be keeping tabs on the weather, but if you feel it's too cloudy, even in the slightest, you call me. Do you understand?"

"Yes," he replied, annoyed that the weather reports were predicting a 15 percent chance of rain. "But I don't want to be treated specially."

"You are a special case, Newton. That's the reality. Accept your nature and accept nature herself."

"I—I will, sir."

"Good luck, then."

Mr. Dumont strode into the pack of students, who parted like sheep before a sasquatch. He cleared his throat. "Welcome to the first of four Expeditions you will experience this year. I expect you to spend forty-eight hours surviving on your own in the wild. That is part of your test. We have studied. We have practised. Now it's time for action. I've given you each a walkie-talkie that's to be used for dire emergencies. Or if you find the talisman."

"How do we find it?" Violet asked. "Where do we begin?"

Newton gave her an appraising glance. With her backpack on tight and her hair tied back, she looked ready to sprint into the bush and massacre squirrels.

"The answers to your questions will become clear to you during your trials. Once you have grasped the talisman, return it to its position and come back here. You may proceed using any means necessary."

Any means necessary. That said to Newton that he might have to fight for the talisman. If so, he was ready.

"That is all I will tell you. Now, you must use your wits and what nature provides. And be sure to write your observations in your field journals." Mr. Dumont dumped his jug of water out onto the ground. "No one can take any water with them. Obviously, your first goal will be to find some. You have forty-eight hours, starting now."

"But . . . where do we go?" Jacob asked.

Mr. Dumont ignored his question. "Anyone still standing here in the next thirty seconds will lose five marks."

The class scattered. Newton ran northwest into the brush.

"Hey, Newton!" Jacob called after him. "Newton, wait up!"

He looked over his shoulder. What could Jacob want? This wasn't about teamwork, for heaven's sakes. It was about survival.

Newton sped up, even though his stomach was knotted with guilt. He was certain he'd get better marks if he worked on his own.

"Newton! Newton!" As Newton disappeared into the brush, Jacob's voice faded away.

After running through the dense forest for several minutes, Newton stopped at a ravine and looked around to be sure no one was following him. He trudged up a hill and through more thick brush. He sweated profusely in the noon-hour heat. The knot refused to leave his stomach. But he had to keep going. *It's a contest, Newton. It has nothing to do with friendship.*

Hoping he was far enough away from everyone, he collapsed on a fallen log and opened his backpack. Josephine wriggled out. She sniffed around in a circle, rolled her eyes, and settled down on her tummy with her tail end towards him, trembling.

"Hey, girl," Newton said. "Glad to have you along."

Dumont had said "by any means necessary." No one had mentioned that you couldn't bring your pig.

Newton wondered if he was cheating by bringing along a pig who had a knack for finding things, but he reasoned that since Polynesians used to take pigs on their boats because the animals could smell land, Josephine's presence was no different than carrying a compass.

Well, here I am. Alone. Surviving. So far so good.

He looked at Josephine, who seemed to ignore him. "We're gonna do just fine." She turned away from him again and raised her snout in the air. Clearly she was miffed about having spent so long in his backpack, stuffed in the compartment under the bus.

He looked in the pack to be sure she hadn't left any surprises there. Not a drop or a stinky pebble.

"Now, how do you think we find that talisman before

everyone else?" he said as he picked her up. She rolled her eyes again and let out a great huff.

Newton sighed and began walking, just to feel as though he was doing something. Somewhere out there was the talisman, and it had his name on it.

Surviving Is Fun Until . . .

After two hours of boredom Newton's stomach began to rumble: he'd had overcooked porridge in the mess at eight that morning and it was now sometime after two. He decided to go deeper into the forest. He'd find water, build his shelter, then hunt for food. In the shadows of the pine trees he thought he heard a twig snap. A fellow student? Or worse, a coyote or bobcat? They wouldn't be a bother for him, but they'd probably like a taste of Josephine. He resolved to keep a close eye on her.

She stopped to smell a pine cone, then a mushroom. "Reliving truffle-hunting season?" he asked. She nodded quite deliberately. He did a double-take, but she was back to sniffing at the ground. *You're hallucinating, Newton. You haven't had enough to eat.*

After another hour of climbing and sweating, his pack felt as if it were full of stones. He checked his *sgian dubh* to be sure it was still in its sheath, the familiar handle reassuring. "Lads and lassies, check your knife every second step," Mr. McBain had drilled into them. "It should become a natural reflex!" Newton chastised himself for not checking it often enough.

Where the pine trees gave way to a few poplars, he came across a small clearing (he knew the inside of the poplar bark was edible and could be made into a tea). Newton set his pack down next to a tree where the grass was quite green. There was no obvious source of water.

He swallowed. His tongue was dry. He didn't remember seeing any streams and he wasn't sure if he had the energy to go looking for one. He knew it took three days for a human being to die of dehydration.

Newton spotted a goldfinch. In class he'd learned that if it flew away straight and low it was heading for water, though it only drank at dusk and dawn, so it would be a while. He squinted up at the sun. Two-ish or so.

He looked at Josephine. Josephine looked at him.

"Would you find me some water, please?" he asked.

She rolled her eyes, got to her feet, and sniffed along the ground and across the clearing. He followed her.

They walked for three or four minutes before she stopped in front of a creek, its source somewhere above them in the hills.

He rubbed her back. "You're a life-saving pig."

The water tasted like heaven. He and Josephine drank and drank. He filled his canteen.

As he wiped the water from his chin, an unsettling thought came to Newton: *I could have done this on my own. If only I'd had a bit more patience.*

He shook his head. It wasn't really cheating to use her, he decided. *She's just another tool in my toolbox.*

He sat back on his haunches. *Okay, time to locate me some calories. Since normal activities burn 115 calories an hour, I need 2,760 calories to keep my motor running. Maybe a couple thousand more to replace the energy I used getting here. So at least 4,000 in total.*

He turned on his survival eyes, and next to an anthill he found several wild onions. He dug them out of the soft soil and ate them quickly. They were one-twelfth the size of normal onions and tasted a little sweet, but they still stung his eyes as he peeled them. He dug around for more food, then wrote it all down in his field journal:

I consumed the following:

Wolf willow fruit
Dandelion leaves
Cow parsnip shoots
Two handfuls of chokecherries
A handful of dried Saskatoon berries

Newton decided shelter was next on his list. He found a young, slender fallen poplar and tied it between two pine trees, using bark strips. Then he tied pine branches to the pole and created an A-frame lean-to. It took longer than he'd expected to finish. The whole time, the phrase *You're only as sharp as your knife* went around and around in his head like a miniature train set. He was covered with sap, had several painful slivers, and wished he'd brought work gloves.

He sat inside his masterpiece and wrote a report on the whole experience. Josephine nibbled on an acorn. When he was done, he smiled. He'd truly accomplished something today.

Not a Silent Night

After spending the rest of the day making short, fruitless excursions from his base camp, hoping to stumble across the talisman, Newton watched the sun set and the night settle in. The park was big; he hadn't seen or heard any of his classmates. It was clear and cold, and it wasn't long before the coyotes began calling to each other, their eerie voices howling as if from another world.

He knew Jacob was somewhere out there listening to the same sounds. At that moment he wished he could talk with him.

Newton changed into his pants. It would take some time for his legs to warm up. He began to shiver and slid himself into his sleeping bag, with one arm over Josephine, who had made her own bed of grass. He gently laid a small towel over her.

He hadn't been outdoors alone for this long ever before in his life. He couldn't help but review his situation, his mind getting stuck on two things.

The first: his mother's untimely death. Fate had been cruel to her, to his family, snatching her away while she was still so young. Why did she have to be outside on that day, anyway?

The second: When would he die? The lightning was always looking for him, waiting for the right moment to strike, the right conditions to take him down.

When sleep finally came, it was fitful.

A Motherly Memory

"Mom."

In the night he awoke. His dreams swirled around and around, then were sucked down his mental drain.

Crickets. The rustling of a few fall leaves. Josephine was snoring lightly. *Did I shout something? Was that me?*

His mother. She'd been in his dream. But it was more than that. It was a memory of his first awareness that he was a Starker, and all the fear the name carried with it.

He'd been four years old, looking out the door at the falling rain. There were children playing just outside the dome. He could see them jumping in puddles through the screen door. It looked like fun.

But his mother held him back. "You can't go outside, Newton."

"Why, Mommy?"

"Because the lightning lives in the sky and it will strike you down and kill you and you will die. The lightning is very dangerous for the Starker family. We must always be watchful, Newton. We have to know when the sky is right. Only then can we go outside."

Newton backed away from the door.

His mother picked him up, then held him to her. He would forever remember the way she smelled, her beautiful grey and blue eyes. "Don't worry, Newt," she said, "I'll always protect you. Always."

Wide awake, under a star-studded sky, Newton felt a surge of anger that threatened to suffocate him. His mother had lied to him. She had lied.

The Following Morning

Newton was still shivering. Judging by the frost that he scraped off his eyebrows it had dropped to a few degrees above freezing. *Okay, Newton. Time to take on the world.* He steeled himself for the cold and jumped out of his sleeping bag, quickly pulling on his kilt over his pants. It was a look, anyway. He jogged in a circle and Josephine followed him, leaves crunching under their feet.

He gathered a few branches and built a small fire. He warmed his hands, then made a sludgy tea in his Sierra cup from stinging nettle leaves. It took six minutes of boiling to destroy the formic acid in the hairs on the leaves but, according to Mr. McBain, there were plenty of nutrients in the plant. The tea had tasted rather horrendous when they'd made it in culinary class. In the real outdoors, it was even worse.

He had a sudden craving for eggs Benedict. Then, when Josephine rubbed her snout on his ankle, he felt an immediate stab of guilt. When her eyes met his, he was compelled to say, "I wouldn't have it with ham. Maybe I'll switch to eggs Florentine. No bacon, just spinach."

She oinked twice.

Newton wasn't sure what that meant. Nor did he know what to do. Were they supposed to just wait around? And how was he to know what the talisman was? Maybe the whole Expedition was intended as a vision quest, and the form and location of the talisman would appear in his head.

After a minute or two of attempting to visualize the talisman, all he could see was a Philly cheese steak sandwich.

He and Josephine started walking. By early afternoon he was feeling a little dizzy and he found it hard to think straight. *It's because I haven't had any meat.* He recalled what he'd learned in Culinary Arts: *A snake is a steak.* Yes, snakes would be a good meal. But then he remembered that garter snakes were all they had around the Cypress Hills, and the odd rattler, neither of which provided much meat.

An odd voice turned on in his head. Sometimes it seemed like his own, but more often it seemed higher in pitch and a little rangy.

There'll be rabbits out here somewhere. What's the best way to catch one? Right, a snare. A snare! But a snare requires patience and time and, oh, the actual snare. I'm hungry now. In any case, rabbit meat doesn't have enough nutrients. People starve to death if they just eat rabbits. One rabbit would be good, though. Maybe a Richardson's ground squirrel would be better. I could make stew with the onions and a little truffle. A properly prepared truffle would be perfect right now. Or another meal at Nit's—those chicken sticks, perhaps. Are there wild chickens in the Cypress Hills? I could steal the chickens from a farm. No, theft wouldn't get me a good mark.

Think small. I know it's not natural for you, but think small.

He lifted up several stones and caught two crickets, removed their wings, antennae, and leg spurs, then tossed them in his mouth. They crunched and their bug guts squished out, a bitter taste mixed with a smidgen of shrimp.

Under another rock he found a large beetle, which he plucked from the ground and dropped in his mouth. He tried to distract his brain by counting pebbles, hoping to fool himself into thinking he wasn't actually going to swallow the thing. After two quick, crushing bites he tasted the oddest apple-like flavour, then swallowed the shattered, gunky remains. *They have good food value; rich in fat, protein, and carbohydrates. And they're easy to catch.*

He spent a good portion of the afternoon leaning against a pine tree, sipping from his canteen, arms across his stomach, wincing. Had the beetle been poisonous? Or had he not actually killed it, and it was now charging around his stomach?

Josephine slept at his feet, awakening occasionally to trot around in a circle or chase a moth. Somehow her skin was a warmer pink colour. Being out in nature was kind of like watching TV, the colours were more vivid.

By late afternoon the stomach pain had subsided and he grew hungry again. He returned to his camp and started another fire. He found several earthworms, which he roasted on a green stick. They tasted a lot like charcoal.

He chewed another green stick to a pulp in lieu of using a toothbrush (which he'd forgotten to bring). Then he went to bed. Lying there under his lean-to, once again he was troubled, but not so much by his doomed life as by the apparent uselessness of the Expedition. He had the feeling he'd missed some important clue.

Newton Starker's Chocolate Cricket Recipe

Collect two dozen crickets. Wash them in a covered colander. Shake them dry. Place them in the freezer for 15 minutes to kill them (but don't let them freeze). Remove the head, hind legs, and wing cases (if you don't want them to get stuck in your teeth). Bake at 250°F until they are deliciously crunchy. Dip the crickets in melted semi-sweet chocolate (you'll need several squares) and let cool on wax paper. Enjoy!

A Sudden Announcement Well Past the Witching Hour

"Attention, students of the Jerry Potts Academy, this is Mr. Dumont."

The voice made Newton shake himself out of sleep. He opened his eyes to darkness and the hooting of owls. For a moment he believed the owls had spoken. When the message was repeated, he couldn't make sense of it. Mr. Dumont was talking to them from the heavens.

Then Newton remembered the walkie-talkie. He wiggled out of the sleeping bag and dug the radio from his backpack.

"I will tell you this only once. The talisman is under the plough north of the swan, and it's hairless. You may now find the talisman, using any means necessary."

Newton shook his sleepy head. Under the plough? The swan? Hairless? None of it made sense. He heard crickets chirping and wondered if the sound was coming from inside his head . . . or his stomach.

The plough. What could that be? Had he passed a plough on the way here? What could the swan mean? And hairless?

Hairless?

Violet probably already has it figured out. He thought his brain would explode from thinking so hard. *She's closing in on the talisman at this very moment!* He quickly buckled on his kilt and shoved his pants to the bottom of the backpack. *Mr. Dumont might frown on pants.*

He'd think better if he got moving and sent some fresh blood to his brain. He packed up camp, threw on his backpack, and started stumbling in no particular direction. Josephine followed, blinking away sleep.

He spun the puzzle around and around in his head. For all he knew, he could be moving farther away from the prize. *Plough. Swan. Hairless. Any means necessary.* It sounded very military.

He'd already been trudging along through the night for at least twenty minutes when it occurred to him that he might be going in a circle.

Then he looked down at Josephine.

"Josephine," he said, very softly, "please find the talisman for me."

She raised one ear and looked at him, as if to say, "Are you sure?" That was his chance to say no, to change his mind and figure it all out on his own. *This is cheating. No, Dumont said "any means necessary." No qualifiers. Maybe I'll get extra marks for bringing a pig with a sixth sense and a compass for a brain.*

"Please," he said. "Please, Josephine."

She let out a soft oink and, sure enough, turned to walk in the opposite direction.

Excerpt from *The Survival Handbook of the Jerry Potts Academy*

At night, everything becomes the unknown. Disorientation and a feeling of being lost can easily overcome you. Fight against this. Look at the edges of objects, not the dark mass in the middle. The edges catch the light. The edges will show you the way.

The Swan Song

Newton followed Josephine. The stars twinkled through the tree branches. He felt as though he were floating just above the ground. This was the right thing to do, he was on the right path.

He entered a large clearing and the stars shone brilliantly over them. He picked out the Big Dipper immediately, then the Northern Cross. Its position indicated that he was heading north. He was thrilled. The lessons from class had stuck to his brain like flies to flypaper.

Then he recalled Mr. Dumont's words: "The talisman is under the plough north of the swan . . ." Somewhere in the recesses of his grey matter these words began to ring a bell. Yes—it was from one of his classes. Something a teacher had said in passing. Newton rubbed his temples. The Plough was another name for the Big Dipper! And the Swan was also the Northern Cross. So he *was* going in the right direction! Soon he'd come to a hairless place. That bit still confused him. He scratched his head. Hair. Hairless. Shaved. Did it have something to do with a monk? Monk's Hill? Did that exist?

Hairless. Bald! Hey, maybe it was Bald Butte! He'd read about the lookout point at the top of the Cypress Hills. That was it! He didn't need Josephine after all.

"Ha," he said to himself. "Ha!" he yelled to the forest.

Josephine looked back at him but kept marching forward and he followed. *No sense letting her know.*

After climbing uphill through another long stretch of pine trees into the open, they were hit by a sharp blast of wind. Newton stopped, huffing and puffing. He recognized the place as Bald Butte only because they were so high he could feel it in the coolness of the air in his lungs. The view was breathtaking, the sky aglitter with stars, the moon a sliver of a smile. The wind tousled his hair.

Josephine led him on right to the top, and they looked around. There seemed to be nothing of significance. Then he saw something very small glowing up ahead.

He made a run for it and, just as suddenly, fell.

"Sorry, Newt," Violet said. Newton looked up from the dirt as she charged on ahead of him. He pushed himself to his feet and was at her heels when she reached for the object—a cellphone, set on top of a large stone.

Newton tackled her and they rolled a few yards down the hill. Josephine oinked after them. He'd never heard her go on like that. Whether she was cheering him on or scolding him he couldn't say.

"You brought your pig?" Violet exclaimed.

"Any means necessary," Newton growled as she kicked him and broke free. He wasn't sure exactly what happened next. They both scrambled up the hill to the phone, but Violet lost her footing and tumbled into the darkness.

Newton grabbed the cellphone, opened it. He pressed a blinking button and it dialled automatically.

"Congratulations," Mr. Dumont said into his ear. "Return the cellphone to its perch for the next student to find and proceed down the hill to the bus."

Newton swept up Josephine, stuffed her in his backpack, and started down the hill. The bus had been parked northeast of the Butte. He guessed it to be about a twenty-minute jog.

"Newton!" Violet screamed. "Newton! I think I've broken my leg."

"Ha!" Newton yelled. "I'm not falling for that."

"I'm not kidding, Newt. Oww. Ahh. I'm not kidding."

Right. Any means necessary, including trying to trick me.

He carried on down the hill towards the thickening bush.

Into the Gathering Darkness

He ran, victorious, through the dark, dodging trees and lifting his feet high over the underbrush. His spirit soared, picturing the Hall of Heroes, but soon guilt, angst, and fear began flapping around in his mind like buzzards. *What if she really does have a broken leg? What if she's bleeding?* Violet was mean, but she hadn't thrown the stone that made his kilt fall. Newton had started their conflagration by spilling porridge on her. Violet had tried to call a truce. He'd rejected it.

But most important, Violet didn't seem like the type who would lie. She might take some pleasure in knocking him out in a fistfight, but lying—that wasn't part of her modus operandi.

Newton skidded to a stop, lost his balance, and fell into wet leaves and roots poking up from the ground. He caught his breath. He thought of Jacob, how he'd run away from him. Perhaps they could have found the talisman together and shared in the glory. And now he was leaving Violet behind, and worse, she might be seriously injured.

She had left him a rose when he'd been injured.

He hung his head. That decided it. He would go back.

The problem was—in the dark he had no idea which way he was facing. The forest blocked the stars, not one was visible. He squinted at the sky and shivered.

Josephine oinked.

"Of course!" he said. "My friend, my friend, I hear you."

He let her out of his backpack and she shook herself like a dog.

"Find Violet."

She oinked repeatedly and rubbed at her nose with her foot. Her eyes were glowing strangely.

"Please," he added.

Josephine nodded and sped off to his right. He followed the gleam of light on her pink skin.

Twice he nearly brained himself on pine branches. Josephine was taking the most direct path—perfect for pigs, not so good for humans. He held his head and charged on after her, once again ascending towards Bald Butte.

For a short while Josephine disappeared completely. Panic in his heart, Newton stood still as a statue until he heard a rustling. He ran towards it, a branch scratching him just below the eye, and finally caught a glimpse of Josephine's glowing pink skin. There was a squawking in his backpack. Mr. Dumont was using the walkie-talkie, but it was buried in the bottom. And Newton didn't want to stop now.

As they got closer to the top Newton's legs began to shake. He was sweating. There was something about the air—it seemed suddenly warmer; maybe it was just his physical exertion. The hairs on his arms and along the back of his neck began to stand up. He knew that feeling only too well, and so it was no surprise when, five seconds later, lightning flashed in the distant sky, turning the world white. He immediately began to count.

"One . . . two . . . three . . . four . . . five . . . six—"

A roll of thunder boomed through the wood so loudly it cracked tree branches. He divided the number of seconds he'd counted by five. The lightning was just over two miles away.

Death was two miles away.

Newton froze. His heart pounded. He listened and waited. Another bang and roll from the angry sky.

He was in the trees! Breaking rule number eight! He threw himself to the ground, landing on sharp pine cones and decomposing leaves. He spread out his arms and legs and hugged the ground like it was a loved one he hadn't seen for years, like it was his mother.

The Light Is Not the End of the Tunnel

He was a mole, burrowing into the ground. *Deeper, mole, deeper. Away from the sky. The night.* His body convulsed with fear. He was flailing his arms at the earth, clawing at the dirt.

It flashed again and he jumped. Thunder three seconds later, the storm was getting closer. He wracked his brain, trying to think of a way to get to a safer place.

The wind was howling in the treetops. In the noise of the storm he thought he heard a laugh, a cackle, really. *I told you so, Newton.* It was his great-grandmother's voice. *Spite. Spite is what you need to survive.*

Spite? How about fear? He needed to get back to the bus and huddle in the middle, away from the metal sides. The lightning would run down the sides into the ground. With the windows closed, the bus was where he would be absolutely safe. But how to get there? It all seemed so impossible. He collapsed in a heap and wrapped his arms around his knees.

He just had to find the strength to go back there.

Josephine poked him in the head and oinked. She was peering down at him. How was it possible for a face to look so angelic and so porcine at the same time?

"Find the bus," he pleaded. "Find the bus."

But she just stood there staring at him.

"You silly pig, find the bus," Newton hissed.

He was frightened by the sound of his voice. Josephine backed off two steps and lay down. What was he supposed to do now? And that's when the rain began, soaking him through, making him an even better conductor.

Is this how Mom died? Huddled in fright on the ground, close to safety but not close enough?

"You said you'd always protect me," he whispered. "You promised." He wanted to sink into the earth, be done with it all.

"*Oink*," Josephine said softly. She trotted over and nudged his knee.

No. Newton realized he was not alone. He had his father. Josephine. Jacob.

And what about Violet? If her leg really was broken then she was stranded in the rain. Alone. She was no safer under a tree than he was. He didn't want to be remembered for leaving another human being alone.

Just as he stood up the thunder roared again. This time he didn't bother counting.

"Find Violet!" he yelled over the din. "Please!"

Josephine turned and began to run back up Bald Butte. Lightning flashed nearby. There was another *crack*, then a *crackle* right behind him. He didn't look back, he just scampered on through the slick leaves. His kilt, heavy with water, slapped against his muddy knees and threatened to slip down over his bony hips.

Josephine led him back to the area where he and Violet had tumbled together.

"Violet!" he screamed through the storm. He picked up Josephine and held her close. She was ice-cold. "Violet, where are you?"

"Newton!" Violet shouted from the dark. "I'm here! Over here!"

He followed her voice till he could see a dark shape up against a tree.

"You came back," she said.

In a flash of lightning he saw her determined eyes and chattering teeth. Her hair and clothes were soaked.

"Your leg—it's really broken?"

"Yes. I dragged myself up here to get out of the mud."

"You're a tough one."

"I know."

"If you set it yourself you'll get extra marks."

She laughed, and for a tiny moment Newton's breath caught in his throat, and he knew he was happy to be with her. He put Josephine down and guided Violet's arm awkwardly over his shoulder, then put his arm around her small waist. She leaned on him. As she lifted her injured leg, he felt her flinch.

"I thought you hated me," she said, her breath passing over his ear. He looked up at her, thinking she wasn't quite so tall after all.

"I thought I did too. But now I know you didn't make my kilt drop."

She forced a sly smile. "I'll think of something far more evil to do to you."

They were silent for a second, and she bent her head a little to kiss him on the cheek. He froze, surprised and frightened, having never been kissed by a girl other than his mother. But somehow it felt like the obvious thing to do. The sensation was amazing, an electrical current running from her lips to his heart and all over his skin, until his hair stood on end.

Then thunder cracked and he realized why he was feeling so electric. He pushed Violet away and she staggered, trying not to fall.

"Newton!" she yelled, "What are you doing?"

"You're in danger!" he shouted. "Get down!" He ran like a maniac. He had to get farther away, then she would be safe. He heard a series of oinks coming from right behind him. "Go away," he shouted over his shoulder at Josephine. "Go away! Please!"

A great *boom* like an explosion shook the ground. A jagged bolt of lighting crossed the night sky and cut a line straight down, directly into the top of Newton's head.

A Striking Moment

It took only a microsecond for three hundred kilovolts to pass through him, but that was time enough, it seemed, to experience a hundred different images and sensations, among them feeling his hair shoot straight out; feeling his heart beat hard, then stop; seeing everything around him fade to white.

His body was made of cotton. Two neon figures floated in front of him and several above him. *Newton, Newton, Newton.* This was his mother's voice. *You aren't supposed to be here now. Not yet. Not yet.* And then another, older, ragged voice whispered, *He's still cross-eyed.*

The lightning continued to burn through his brain, his arteries, his muscles—forcing all of them to contract.

What does it mean? Why us? he asked.

He's still whining.

One creature of light moved closer. Was that his mother's face? Yes! Her eyes, blue and grey, sparkled. *It's a stage. That's all. A stage of the journey. So don't let yourself be ruled by fear. Let it all pass through you.*

She was already fading.

No. Mom. Don't leave me.

She disappeared, and Newton felt his life being dragged out of his body as the current escaped through a hole at his ankle. He would die alone.

Mr. Dumont's words came back to him: *Mother Nature has more mysteries up her sleeve than we'll ever understand. We can only let her flow through us.*

At that split second something touched his ankle. He couldn't move a muscle to look, but he knew it was Josephine. She rested her head across his foot, letting the charge enter her body, straightening her tail.

The lightning left Newton and he fell, smoking, to the ground. A sizzling bacon smell entered his nostrils. It took all his strength to turn to Josephine. She smiled a half-smile and oinked gently, then closed her eyes.

Excerpt from *The Survival Handbook of the Jerry Potts Academy*

Survival is not about being unafraid. People who don't feel fear are unnatural. The key to survival is acknowledging your fears. Accept that you will feel afraid and act in spite of it.

The Aftermath

Newton awoke to about ten faces looking down on him, the pale sky of sunrise behind them. One of them was Violet's. She was leaning on Mr. Dumont. Next to her was Jacob. Newton blinked. His mouth tasted like battery acid. He spat and everyone ducked, then returned to gawk at him some more. Some of their mouths were moving. *I can't hear you. I can't HEAR you.*

He couldn't seem to open his mouth. His teeth ached as though he'd been punched in the jaw. His right ear popped. Then his left.

"Hey, there's a pig over here," someone said.

"*Jo-seph-ine?*" Newton rasped, his lips now functioning. "*Jo-seph-ine?*"

"Who?" asked Mr. Dumont.

"She's—I'm afraid she's not moving, Newt," Jacob said. "Looks like she got jolted, too."

Mr. Dumont leaned in and sat Newton upright. "We'll get you home, son," he promised. Newton blinked, tried to process the information. His head throbbed wildly.

"*Bring Jo-seph-ine,*" he slurred, looking around for her. Jacob skipped over a few feet and brought the pig back, cradled in his arms.

Newton could barely raise an arm to touch her. She moved her leg, let out a soft, "*Oink*."

It sounded to Newton like, "I told you so."

After the Aftermath

Newton remembered little about the ride. Mr. McBain drove the bus while Mr. Dumont watched over him the whole way, a grave look on his face. Newton faded in and out of consciousness.

"Where are we going?" he asked, during one of his more lucid moments.

"Maple Creek."

"Oh. Good."

Darkness. Light. Darkness. Then: "I found the talisman."

"Yes, you did."

"Was . . . was I first?"

Mr. Dumont's expression didn't change. "No. You and Violet were last."

Despite his difficulties, Newton had no trouble processing this news; it was a shock of another order. "Last? But . . . how did . . . ?"

Mr. Dumont's eyes met his and twinkled. "Everyone else worked as a team."

"Oh. How . . . dumb of us . . ." Newton mumbled as he embraced the next spell of darkness.

The next time he came to, he was outside on a stretcher, being wheeled towards a very small hospital.

"Lad," Mr. McBain said, his voice tender, "you wear the kilt well."

Newton smiled his euphoria. It was the greatest compliment he'd ever been given.

When he opened his eyes again a doctor with a South African accent was saying, "We'd better send him in an ambulance," and, as though his words made the ambulance appear in a flash, Newton was on his way to Moose Jaw Union Hospital.

For the rest of the day he slept.

Early that evening his father arrived and sat at his bedside. They spoke little.

When Newton was feeling well enough, he asked, "Dad, could you help me out of bed?" and, leaning on his father, he staggered to the washroom so he could look in the mirror. Where the lightning had hit him, his hair was burnt to the skull. His eyes were black, as though he'd been in a fistfight. Generally, he looked like death. Every last muscle was tired, as if he'd been stretched on a medieval torture machine.

"I saw Mom," Newton said, matter-of-factly. "I know this'll sound weird, but I saw Mom."

His dad tightened his grip on his arm. "In a dream?"

"No. While I was being struck by lightning. She was there."

His dad's eyes grew large as he mulled this over.

"I don't expect you to believe me," Newton said. "I—I've been thinking about her a lot. Why was she out on the day she died?"

His father looked down at the floor. "I think it was my fault, Newt. I—I forgot to switch the calendar over. She didn't know it was lightning season."

Newton felt suddenly light. He might just have floated away if his father hadn't been holding him.

"I've been meaning to tell you," his dad continued. "I didn't want you to blame me."

"It's not your fault, Dad. It's no one's fault. It's just a mistake. Maybe we should be happy she was going out. Just for a walk. To be outside."

"Maybe," his father said.

"I . . . I don't know how to explain this, either. I let the lightning pass through me. And I think that's why I'm still here. That and . . ." He paused. "Where's Josephine?"

"Who?"

"My pig. Josephine."

His father's eyes lit up. "Oh, right. The pig. Yes, your friend Jacob is looking after her. You aren't supposed to have pets at the Academy, you know."

Newton's face muscles were bruised and sore, but for Josephine, he somehow managed a smile. "She's alive? Alive? Fantastic!"

His father helped him back into bed. "Newton, I should've watched you more closely."

"It's okay, Dad," he replied. "It's out of our hands. Really, it is. Totally out of our hands."

Burning the Midnight Oil

Newton slept and slept until he felt something poke his forehead. Lightning? His eyes popped open and, lying on his side, he found himself face to face with Violet. She was entertaining herself by tapping a pen on his skull. She sat in a wheelchair, a cast on her right leg.

"It's about time you woke up," she said. "I've been here twenty minutes. I got bored and decided to speed up the process."

"Oh," Newton said, and scoped the room for his father. He must have left. "How are you?"

"I've been worse. Well, not much worse. But it sure is boring here, isn't it? Aren't hospitals boring? Are you bored?"

"Right now," he said, "no."

That got a smile. "Thanks for coming back for me," she said.

"I should've stayed in the first place. I should've believed you."

"Yep, you should have. Don't I have a believable face?" She grinned. Newton decided he liked her smile.

"You do. I just didn't see it before."

Violet nodded. "Anyway," she said, "I just wanted to be sure you were all right. That you have all your faculties. I worried that the lightning might've fried your sense of humour." She paused. "By the way, you've got really cool eyes. Catch you soon." Violet spun around in her wheelchair and rolled out the door, leaving Newton speechless.

She likes my eyes.

He looked to the bedside table for his glass of water and broke into a grin. A single rose smiled back at him.

Then from down the hall someone shouted, "Ouch!" to which he heard Violet reply, "Hey! Watch where you're going!"

A moment later Jacob came limping in, one hand on his knee. "Violet ran over my foot."

Newton laughed. "It's probably best to not get in her way. I've learned that."

"So, the phoenix has risen," Jacob said.

It took Newton a second to figure out that Jacob was referring to him.

"How are you feeling?"

"I ate crickets."

Jacob nodded. "We caught a couple of rabbits and made a fabulous stew. Too bad you didn't stick with us."

"Yeah, not one of my smartest moments. I'm sorry I ran off on you like that."

"Ah, worry not, my friend. I don't hold a grudge. By the way, they didn't want me to bring Josephine. There's a No Pets policy here."

"Tell her I miss her," Newton said.

"Oh, tell her yourself." He stepped back around the door

frame and reappeared with the pet carrier. "I couldn't just leave her in your room."

He flipped open the door and Josephine shot out like a bright pink jack-in-the-box. She bounded across the bed, landing on Newton's chest. She rubbed her nose on his chin. "Josephine!"

"*Oink. Oink. Oink. Oink!*" she squealed, dancing in a circle on his stomach. Like Newton's, the top of her head was burned where the lightning had struck her.

Newton smiled. "Thank you, Josephine," he said. "Thank you for everything."

The Big Goodbye

Three days later, Newton's dad took him by cab to the Academy to pack up. There wasn't much: three kilts, four shirts, undershorts, civilian clothing, his laptop, a few books and toiletries. He lifted his mother's picture and drawing from the wall and packed them carefully in the folds of his kilts. He took a moment to don a clean one.

"All done," he said, surveying the spartan room. His father had Josephine's pet carrier.

Mr. Dumont rapped on the door as he stepped in. "Ah, already packed." He lifted the suitcase easily. "I'm sorry, you're going to miss a quarter of your classes this year. You can make them up later; you're a quick study. It's more important that you recuperate fully. Take all the time you need. Most people can't walk for weeks after being struck by lightning."

He handed Newton a thick, leather-bound book. Newton looked at the cover: *The Survival Handbook of the Jerry Potts Academy.* It was surprisingly heavy. He could have knocked out a bull with it. "My very own copy?"

"Yes. And I expect you to study it carefully while you're away." He lifted an eyebrow. "I just have to ask, Newton: Why did you bring a pig with you on the Expedition?"

"The Polynesians used pigs on their boat trips. They could smell land. Josephine helped me find water. Actually, she found everything," Newton said, somewhat sheepishly.

Doubt filled Mr. Dumont's eyes. "Well, very curious. Creative, too. But it did give you an advantage over the other students."

Oh, here it comes. The punishment I deserve.

"We'll add an extra week of kitchen duty to your schedule upon your return. And you'll have to leave your pig at home next term."

Josephine oinked.

"She'll be good company for me," said Newton's dad.

"That sounds fair," Newton said, picking up Josephine. "Thanks, Mr. Dumont."

Mr. Dumont walked them down the stairs and out into the courtyard, then bade them farewell.

While Newton and his dad were waiting for their cab, Jacob came running out of the dorm.

"Sorry I'm late. I wanted to get this for you." Jacob handed Newton a folder stuffed with paper. "It's a printout of my new novel. You might enjoy it. And I've signed it. If I become really famous you can sell it on eBay."

"Thank you, Jacob." Newton opened the folder and was relieved to see that the novel wasn't one long sentence. "I'll start reading it on the plane."

"How long will you be gone?"

"A few weeks. The doctors want me to rest. And there'll be some tests and such. I'll e-mail you as soon as I'm home."

"Take care, my friend," Jacob said as the cab pulled up. They shook hands, then Newton pushed his hand aside to give him a quick hug. Jacob looked pleased.

By the time Newton was in his seat, a crowd of kilted students had gathered. People stared at him or waved hello. Newton was the now-famous boy who'd been struck by lightning and lived to tell about it. That inspired a certain amount of awe. As the cab pulled away he saluted them all.

It was a long, silent flight home. Josephine had been put in the cargo hold. He hoped she wasn't bored.

At one point, while he thought Newton was sleeping, his father put his hand over Newton's. "I'm glad you're coming home alive," he said. "You're a survivor."

Newton's Rules for Survival

20) Remember to smell the roses.
21) Check the weather. Check it again.

Epilogue

On a bright, sunny day during his second week home, Newton walked down Seattle Hill Road with Josephine at his side. He was in a remarkably good mood, considering he'd been carrying around a headache for the last eight days. This was his first long walk since being home, and he'd been feeling cooped up.

He'd checked the weather several times and was pleased that the sun would be out for a few days. This particular part of Snohomish reminded him of the Jerry Potts Academy, and that made him miss Jacob and Mr. Dumont. And Violet. He still hadn't quite figured out where she fit into his life. A friend? More than a friend? She'd been IM-ing him every day. *Best to just let things happen and see where it goes.*

Newton turned off the road at the Marshland Cemetery. He walked through the graveyard, past old stone headstones, some so weathered the names had faded.

His mother's gravestone was in the newer section. It had fresh flowers around it; his father had been there recently. Josephine sniffed at one and let out a cheerful oink.

The headstone read "*Delilah Starker, Much Loved.*" Oddly, at the top of it was a mark, like a burn, as though even in death the lightning wouldn't leave her alone.

You're safe now, Mom. You're safe.

He had imagined he would be sad coming here, that he might even have wept standing at her grave. Instead he was comforted. For him, she wasn't really gone. He had vivid memories of her time on this earth. She had been such a good mother.

"I know how you felt," he said. "I know what it's like to be afraid. I understand. I don't know if we've won or if the lightning will come again. But I'm not afraid of it any more."

Josephine seemed to oink in agreement.

Newton breathed in deeply. There was something in the air, something earthy and irresistible, almost like the scent of truffles.